THE MISPLACED MISS ELOISE

SCHOOL OF CHARM

MAGGIE DALLEN

1

Miss Eloise Haverford's cheeks ached.

Clasping her hands before her, she smiled sweetly at the crowd gathered around her and tried her best to ignore the rapid flutter in her chest.

She truly wished she could blame her racing pulse on dancing or perhaps the tightness of her stays...

However, it was difficult to blame her current discomfort on dancing and stays when she hadn't yet danced at this evening's fête, and her stays were tied the same way they always were, and by a maid who knew precisely what she was doing.

It was only Eloise who did not know what she was about.

Her skin prickled uncomfortably and her ribcage felt like it was caving in. Oh goodness. What was wrong with her? A sweat broke out along her hairline and Eloise swiped a hand quickly, hoping no one noticed.

They didn't. This crowd might have been gathered around her, and she might have been the woman of the hour, considering she was the bride-to-be they were all celebrating this evening...

Yet no one was paying any attention to her. They were all too busy listening to her fiancé, The Earl of Pickington. Lord *Pickington.*

What a name.

A hysterical giggle threatened as her mind summoned a memory of her younger sister Charlotte's reaction to his name.

Charlotte was sweet as could be, but she'd never learned how to hide her emotions, and the title of Pickington had been met with disdain.

So, you're to be Lady Pickington for the rest of your days? Her nose had wrinkled. *But that doesn't suit you at all!*

Charlotte, her mother had said in a warning tone. But Charlotte hadn't seemed to hear. *It's a title better suited to someone covered in scabs or boils or—*

Charlotte! Their mother had finally gotten her to stop, but not before Eloise and their brother Rodrick had lost the battle with laughter.

Eloise's smile faltered now. It had seemed so very silly at the time. Who cared about what one's title sounded like? What mattered was that she was going to be a countess.

She glanced up at the earl at her side. He was old enough to be her grandfather, another fact Charlotte had felt obligated to point out time and again. Wrinkled and withered, with foul breath that made Eloise's eyes water...when he deigned to speak to her.

Most of the time, like right now, he seemed to forget that she was by his side.

She'd like to think that was another side effect of old age. But she wasn't so certain. He was sharp as a whip when it came to talk of politics or gossip or the latest theatrical performance in town.

Perhaps she was just not interesting enough to warrant his attention.

Her insides fell flat as that truth hit the mark. Yes, that was likely it.

Now if Charlotte were here... That was a girl who demanded attention. She fairly crackled with energy and vitality and—

Oh dear. Now she was battling tears as well as this panicky sensation that would not quit.

She truly did miss Charlotte. Her gaze roamed over her fiancé's ornate townhome and all the finely dressed guests. He'd told her it would be an intimate gathering the night before their wedding. A small celebration among close friends and family to mark the occasion.

As she took in the crush around her, well...it did not feel intimate. And if these were friends, they were not *her* friends. Her family was here somewhere, though—minus Charlotte, of course, as she was traveling with her new husband.

But she'd spotted her parents talking with some of their acquaintances, her brother Rodrick was here somewhere, and she'd seen her friend Mary at one point, but she could not find her now, and...and...

And Eloise was certain the air was being sucked out of this room. She drew in a sharp inhale, hoping to get some air in her lungs.

"...isn't that right, my dear?"

She jerked away out of instinct as Lord Pickington's hand came to the small of her back. All eyes were on her and she caught herself before she could recoil completely. She didn't so much as blink when a wave of rancid heat hit her square in the face as Lord Pickington breathed down on her.

What had he asked? Didn't matter.

She smiled brightly and nodded. "Yes, of course, my lord."

And then he turned back to the others and she was once more ignored as the conversation continued without her.

She was never needed for these sorts of interludes.

They'd been engaged for months now so she'd grown accustomed to Lord Pickington's ways. And his expectations. Of which there were few.

He expected her to smile on command and to agree to whatever he said. That was about it. Oh, and look pretty. He'd outright told her that once. *Your job is to look pretty, my dear.* He'd said this with a scowl as they'd taken a turn about her family's drawing room one evening before dinner.

Her mother had informed him that she'd been ill, but he'd insisted on calling upon her, and then had scolded her for not looking her best.

She shoved that memory aside.

Looking pretty she could do. It was really all her mother had ever expected of her as well, so she ought to be used to it.

Her mother. Maybe she could help. She cast a glance in her mother's direction, hoping to catch her eye. Not that she'd be much help, but she might come over and check on her, at least. Or maybe Eloise could find some way to slip off to the private quarters for some air.

That was all she needed. A little air so she could breathe.

But her mother didn't seem to notice her stares, and Eloise's heart slammed harder and harder with each passing second at Lord Pickington's side. Her limbs were twitching with tension and no amount of telling herself to calm down was helping.

Honestly, what was the matter with her?

She normally glided through evenings such as this one without trouble. She'd long ago mastered the art of smiling sweetly and nodding agreeably, even when her mind wandered.

In fact, it was moments like this one that she typically looked forward to the most. These times when she wasn't expected to participate, and so her mind could roam free.

She could take in the party guests around her and conjure up entertaining stories about them.

But this evening, her mind couldn't seem to escape. It was trapped.

She was trapped.

Her heart tripped and raced, beating harder and faster until her pulse was all she could hear.

She needed a moment to catch her breath. Just one.

And then she spotted him. Rodrick. Her older brother was in the corner talking to his friends. Relief washed through her. He would help her find some space. He'd buy her some time, come up with an excuse to cover for her absence so she could...

So she could...what? Sit? Walk?

Breathe?

She didn't know. All she knew was that this wretched night was passing too slowly and too quickly all at once. There seemed to be a clock ticking in the back of her mind.

By this time tomorrow she'd be wed.

A line of sweat trickled down the back of her neck, but it was a chill that made her shiver.

She waited until there was a pause in the conversation before leaning close to Lord Pickington. "Pardon me, my lord. I see my brother and wish to speak with him."

She needn't have even finished. Lord Pickington gave her a muttered assent, seemingly irritated that she'd interrupted him at all.

She slid away from him, and the farther she got, the better able she was to breathe.

Truly, this was problematic. They'd be married in the early afternoon. She shouldn't be so discomfited by her own husband.

She certainly couldn't have this panicky reaction every time he was near.

She fixed her gaze on her brother. He was a tall gentleman, but he looked slight in the midst of his aggressively masculine friends. She recognized them all, though she was not well acquainted with his crowd.

She might have been if things had been different. But from the moment Eloise had come out in society, she'd known she was to marry Lord Pickington. Even before the engagement was official, her future had been laid out for her. They'd only been waiting for Lord Pickington's period of mourning for his late wife to come to an end before making it official.

Because of this, Eloise hadn't had the sort of Season the other girls her age had experienced. Everyone knew she was spoken for and so none of the young eligible gentlemen paid her much notice. They never danced with her or tried to flirt with her or...

Oh what did it matter? So she'd never had the chance to flirt. So what? But as she approached Rodrick and his friends, she was acutely aware that these were the sort of men she would have spent time with if her situation had been different.

As it was, they only knew her as Rodrick's sister. Most likely didn't even remember her name.

Two of the gentlemen seemed to be saying their goodbyes as she drew near. Not surprisingly. The young and handsome Duke of Carver and his cousin, the Marquess of Kalvin, were notoriously dismissive of stodgy formal events such as this one.

But one of Rodrick's friends remained. The Viscount Wycliffe. Her insides twisted and turned with nerves. Which was ridiculous. The man might have a reputation for being arrogant and dismissive, but he was still a gentleman. And her brother's friend.

There was nothing to be afraid of.

But her already tense innards disagreed, her heart choosing that moment to skip and scatter, making her breath catch and her limbs quake.

If she could just find one minute alone with Rodrick to tell him what was happening.

And what is that? How to explain that she was falling apart inside and she knew not why?

She nearly stumbled over her steps as she wove through a group of Lord Pickington's friends. Maybe Rodrick could tell her what was wrong with her. He was a smart fellow, and he'd been engaged even longer than she. Of course, he actually liked his fiancée, Franny. More than liked her, Eloise suspected. Not that he'd ever admitted as much.

"Rodrick." She called his name as she drew near, but it came out breathless.

Why couldn't she draw in air like a normal person? No matter how much she sucked in, she couldn't seem to get enough. And the air tasted hot and bitter. With each new guest who arrived, she was certain the room was closing in on her.

This was ridiculous. She'd never minded crowds before. But then again, she'd never been to a party celebrating her upcoming nuptials before either.

She'd been opposed to this from the start. Wasn't it bad luck to celebrate a wedding before it even occurred? But her mother had waved away her concerns, stating only that this was what Lord Pickington wished and so that was how it would be.

Her father had made a jest about how Lord Pickington wanted to see the faces of his heirs when they saw the fine birthing hips of his latest wife. Her mother had tsked and told him he'd had too much to drink.

Eloise had blanched, her stomach sinking with horror.

Because her father might have been in his cups when he'd said it, and he'd likely been teasing...

But there'd been some truth to it.

Everyone knew why Lord Pickington hadn't wasted a moment finding a new wife after his last had died. His second.

Eloise was to be his third.

A couple stepped in front of her but didn't seem to notice her existence. No one did unless Lord Pickington ordered them to take notice. Otherwise she was invisible.

Just the soon-to-be third wife of a man prone to losing his spouses. Not that she thought he murdered them or anything so melodramatic as that. They'd both died of natural causes.

Charlotte's voice filled her head, a memory of a horrible joke she'd made before leaving for the continent. Someone had mentioned that he'd lost two wives and to Eloise she'd murmured, *they'd been bored to death, no doubt.*

Eloise had swallowed a laugh and had chided her sister gently the way she ought. But right now...

Oh, right now she had to swallow convulsively to fight off a laugh. And not a good laugh.

Not a happy laugh.

No, this was terrifying laughter, the kind that if she let out...

Well, she wasn't sure if she would ever stop. She had a frightening notion that the laugh would continue until it turned into a scream.

She was panting for breath by the time she reached Rodrick's side.

"Why, Eloise," he said with no lack of surprise. "What are you doing here?"

She blinked at him, a wave of hurt unable to be denied.

Seriously? Even her brother was surprised to find her at her own wedding party?

He gave his head a shake and shared a look she could not comprehend with his friend. "Er, pardon. That came out wrong." Rodrick gave her a smile that made the tension within her ease somewhat. It was the same smile all three siblings shared, and one that made her feel like maybe she did have a friend here, after all.

"What I meant was, what are you doing over here with us when your fiancé is over there?" Rodrick's smile was mildly strained and just a little sad. "It seems Pickington hasn't wanted to let you out of his sights all night."

"Yes, well..." She couldn't finish.

Yes, well...this is my lot now.

Yes, well...perhaps that's why I feel like a prisoner.

Yes, well...please save me because I fear I am losing my mind.

She couldn't say any of those things. There was no way to speak frankly now. Not when his friend was standing right there listening.

Listening...and staring.

She blinked with alarm at the intensity of his dark gaze. After an evening being ignored or overlooked, Eloise suddenly felt very, very...seen.

She blinked again, and this time he looked away. Eloise had the irritating idea that she'd just been dismissed. She'd never been this close to the Viscount Wycliffe before. She'd never actually spoken to him or been introduced. For a moment she wondered why he was even here, but then it came to her with a jarring realization. This was one of those heirs her father was referring to.

Not *the* heir—Lord Pickington had a younger brother up north. One he rarely spoke to, according to her father. But this man was a...cousin. Or a nephew? She wasn't entirely sure of his connection, only that he was one in the long line of gentlemen to whom Pickington refused to cede his title.

"Forgive me, Eloise. Allow me to make introductions," Rodrick was saying, now that he'd overcome his shock that she'd dared step away from her betrothed's side. "I'm sure you've heard me talk about my old school chum, Alex," he said. "I present Viscount Wycliffe." To his friend, he added, "And this is my sister who you've heard so much about, Miss Eloise Haverford." Her brother smiled at her. "Though not for much longer."

She couldn't bring herself to return his smile. She felt as though her insides were withering with her brother's every smile.

Of course, he wouldn't understand.

She didn't even understand this overwhelming panic herself. She suspected Charlotte would have, but she wasn't here.

"Lord Wycliffe," she murmured politely. "So glad you could be here with us this evening."

Her smile, she discovered, had miraculously found its way back onto her face. Practice, she supposed.

She waited for Lord Wycliffe to say something in return. A polite remark on her appearance or felicitations on her upcoming nuptials, or—

"Rodrick, I really must be going."

Or nothing. A nod of acknowledgment was all she'd gotten, and it was a slight one at that.

Her jaw clenched with irritation. This was her party, after all. She was the guest of honor. And he couldn't even spare a *good evening*?

Her brother didn't seem to notice his rudeness, or perhaps it was to be expected from this man. "Of course, Alex. I understand. I'm sure you have much to do to prepare for your travels."

Lord Wycliffe's smile was small and rueful, but even that small hint of a smile did much to soften his features. He had a hard look about him. He was tall—taller than Rodrick and nearly a full head taller than Eloise. He was also broad, alarmingly so. But it was the sharp features, the hard cut of his jaw and the hook of his nose, the harsh line of his cheekbones and the unforgiving set of his brows...

All combined, he was...well, handsome.

But not in a nice sort of way. Her brother was less striking, with his sandy-blond hair and his rather plain features, but there was an approachable appeal about him that she was certain his fiancée appreciated.

"You are traveling?" The words popped out of her mouth, not because she was so very interested in Lord Wycliffe's plans, but because she was still irritated by his rude dismissal.

This fête was for her benefit, after all.

Even if she appeared to be an afterthought.

"Yes, Miss Haverford." He turned to her with the sort of resigned patience she'd come to associate with her sister. Or rather, it was the way her parents treated her sister when she was being disruptive or unruly. It was an exaggerated patience intended to let everyone know that *im*patience was imminent.

All Eloise had done was pose a perfectly polite question.

"He leaves for the continent at first light, isn't that right, Alex?" Rodrick said. He was grinning approvingly, and Eloise wondered if Rodrick had ever harbored any hopes of fleeing his duties for a tour of the continent.

If he'd ever had such hopes, she'd never heard about them.

"Yes, well..." Alex looked around them as if seeking out an escape.

Eloise felt her panicky sensation ebbing into something else. Anger. She blinked in surprise.

Now that was surprising. She did not have a temper, everyone knew that. But she clung to irritation because it was such a blessed relief compared to that horrible panicky feeling she couldn't control or convey.

"Well, don't let us stop you," she said with her most gracious smile. "I'm certain my fiancé will understand if you must leave us early to prepare."

His gaze landed on hers again and his brows hitched ever so slightly. Almost as if...

Oh good heavens. Had he forgotten she was standing there?

Her lips parted. She shouldn't be surprised. That seemed to be her lot at parties such as this one. She'd grown used to her parents' friends overlooking her and Lord Pickington ignoring her, but...

Well, this was different. He was Rodrick's friend, and not much older than her. For all that everyone told her how pretty she was, she'd never doubted it so much as right now.

What sort of man *forgot* a pretty woman standing right beside him?

But, she supposed, one could be both pretty and forgettable. And that was her.

She drew in a deep gulp of air as panic set in again so quickly and so forcibly, she nearly clapped a hand to her chest in response.

As it was, she gasped for air. *Rodrick, help me.*

But her brother was looking past her, his eyes bright with pleasure. "Oh, there she is! Eloise, do you mind?" He didn't wait for an answer, already scooting away from her. "I must greet Fanny and her father."

"Yes, of course." But he was gone before she'd finished

answering. And one glance at Lord Wycliffe said he was angling to walk away from her as well.

She glanced around in a panic.

Was there no one here who could see that she was drowning?

Did no one realize she was falling apart right there in the midst of this crowd? She searched for Mary. Her sister's close friend from finishing school had always been good to her. But Mary was dancing with her fiancé, Lord Paul.

And Lord Pickington...

"Oh dear," she whispered. He was coming straight toward her, his gaze narrowed in a glare.

"Miss Haverford, are you all right?" Lord Wycliffe didn't sound concerned so much as...put out. A glance confirmed that he was eyeing her warily.

If scowls could speak, his would say, *please don't fall apart on my watch*. Or something perhaps more eloquent, but no less cutting.

Irritation flared again. Who was he to judge her for falling apart? Did he think she *wanted* to feel like she was dying at her own party?

She turned back to see Lord Pickington weaving his way toward her.

Panic on one side and irritation on the other.

Panic was worse. Far worse.

She turned to Lord Wycliffe with a bright smile. "Did you say you wished to dance?"

His brows drew together. "Pardon? No, I—"

"Of course, I'd love to dance," she answered loudly—far too loudly, in fact—and latching onto an arm he hadn't offered. "How could I say no to you when we are to be family?" she continued just as Pickington reached her side. She turned to her fiancé with a beatific smile. "Isn't that right, Lord Pickington?"

2

Alex knew he shouldn't have come.

"Of course, my dear," Lord Pickington said with a smile that didn't reach his eyes. "Alex will be your family soon enough. It would be good for you to get to know one another."

Alex pressed his lips together to keep them from curling up in a sneer. His uncle was even more vile than he'd remembered, with watery red-lined eyes and wrinkles that seemed to exacerbate his scowls.

But right now, Pickington wasn't scowling. He was gloating.

The old coot had been crowing to anyone who'd listen about how he'd found himself a young wife who came from good stock. When Pickington had been deep in his cups at his cousin's funeral, he'd actually referred to her as a broodmare.

That had been an unseemly moment indeed. A funeral wasn't exactly the place for crowing, and certainly not the occasion to be referring to one's bride-to-be as a beast. Not that there was ever a good time for such a thing.

The sneer was hard to control as Alex met his uncle's gloating gaze.

Truthfully, Alex didn't care if this man sired ten sons. He had no wish to be earl, and besides which, there was another uncle standing between him and the title. An uncle even more abhorrent than this one, if such a thing were possible.

He had no desire for more responsibility than he already shouldered, and the last thing in the world he wanted was to be saddled with the sort of marriage Pickington was about to enter into...for the third time.

Keep your boring, placid little wives and breed as many sons as you like. Just leave me out of it.

But of course, he couldn't say that. And right now, Alex couldn't escape the smug smile without being unutterably rude. Rodrick's sister had cornered him into a dance, and he could see no way out of it without humiliating her in front of Pickington.

He'd often wondered how Pickington's wives had endured him. But then again...they hadn't endured for long, had they?

Unexpected pity reared up as he looked down at this pretty, wide-eyed beauty. So youthful and innocent.

How long would she maintain that smile in his uncle's dour household? How long before she realized her days would begin and end answering to Pickington's commands.

Power-hungry old goat.

"If you'll excuse us," he said to his uncle, angling himself and Miss Haverford toward the dance floor.

Pickington stepped aside, out of their way. "Of course, of course." To Eloise, he added, "I was just on my way to find your father and finalize the arrangements for tomorrow."

She nodded and smiled and...

Was it his imagination or had she gone sickly pale?

Didn't matter. Just so long as she didn't faint while they were dancing.

His jaw tightened in irritation. To think, he'd been one foot out the door and now he had to stay for a dratted dance. "Shall we?" he murmured, leading her away from Pickington.

One dance and then he could leave, he promised himself.

He hated gatherings like this one, all stodgy and formal and filled with people he couldn't stand. He'd only come because Rodrick had invited him, and he'd known this might be his last chance to say farewell to his old school chums before he left for his trip.

He'd meant to come and go within an hour, and then spend the remainder of his evening preparing his journey. He glanced down at the pretty lunatic who clung to his arm.

But now there was this.

She smiled anew when his gaze met hers. His own lips curved down in response. It was rude, he knew, but he couldn't help it. Young ladies like this one...

Well, this right here was a part of the reason he was leaving the country. His uncle could gloat until the end of his days over winning the hand of the renowned beauty, but it wouldn't change the fact that Miss Eloise Haverford represented everything he did not want in his life.

A sliver of ice seemed to travel down his spine as he regarded the simpering smile at that dim, vacant stare. It was the same hollow, yet pleasant expression his mother had worn, right up until her death.

He steeled himself against a wave of that toxic mix of pity and anger he'd come to expect whenever thoughts of his mother surfaced.

The music ended as they approached the dance floor, and just when they reached the other dancers, a waltz began.

Wonderful. Now he'd have to converse with the simpleton.

And clearly she *was* simple. She'd done nothing but smile and ask benign questions in that oddly breathy voice—like she was too frail to speak at a normal decibel. Of course, it likely wasn't her fault. She'd no doubt been trained to speak softly and to only spout meaningless trite.

But whether it was her fault or not, as he drew her into his arms and moved her in time with the music, he found himself actively disliking her all the same.

Whether it was fair or not, he simply couldn't abide simpering young ladies like Miss Haverford.

Even if he did have enough heart left to pity them.

After a few moments of moving gracefully in his arms, she finally broke the silence. "Lord Wycliffe, is there a reason you're glaring at me so?"

Her smile hadn't faltered, and he had a sickening feeling he was staring into the eyes of a porcelain doll. Beautiful and smiling...but empty and soulless.

A shudder went down his spine.

But then her words registered, so at odds with the smile that he found himself frowning anew. "Pardon?"

Now *he* sounded like the simpleton and her smile grew. "I was just wondering if I've done something to offend you."

"Aside from steering me into a dance that I never wished for?"

She had the good grace to blush slightly. "Yes, aside from that."

He studied her closely. Why? Why had she done it? That and her direct question just now were the only signs that perhaps there was more to her than meets the eye.

Not much, perhaps, but she was Rodrick's sister, after all. And Rodrick was quick-witted, as well as good-hearted. Surely, he ought to give Rodrick's sister the benefit of the doubt.

"Apologies," he said stiffly. "I didn't realize I was glaring."

"And my apologies for forcing you into a dance," she shot back quickly. "I do not normally act so...impulsively."

"But tonight you've made an exception?" he asked, trying to keep his voice mild because there was something delicate about her. He feared one harsh word from him and she'd faint. Or worse...cry.

She lifted her shoulders in the daintiest hint of a shrug. "Everyone keeps telling me it's normal to be nervous the night before one's wedding."

It was a statement, but he felt certain there was a question in her eyes. What was he supposed to do? Reassure her that his uncle would make her happy?

If she were that gullible and easy to please, perhaps this was a good match, after all.

In the end, he said nothing at all.

She lowered her gaze and kept it down, as if there was something of great interest on his cravat.

"So, I was a handy escape from your fiancé then, was I?" He meant to sound teasing, but he wasn't in the best of moods, and his attempt fell short.

"I-I suppose so, yes," she said, her blush deepening. "Though we *are* to be related soon—"

"And if you think I'll be referring to you as aunt, you are wrong."

Again, too harsh.

Curse it. This was why he didn't dance with nice young ladies.

There were a whole lot of not-so-nice young ladies out there in the world, and he'd give just about anything to be with one of them right now. Instead, he was holding a porcelain doll who looked like she might break if he looked at her wrong.

"So, I shan't call you my little nephew then, shall I?"

It took a full second for him to realize she was teasing. He let out a reluctant huff of amusement.

"You are his nephew, aren't you? I met most of Lord Pickington's family at a smaller gathering last week but you were not there." She blushed again, and the pink made her startlingly blue eyes seem even brighter. "Of course, you knew that."

"I'm not terribly fond of family gatherings," he said. "Nor parties in general."

She bit her lip. "I see. I'm sorry to have kept you."

He didn't answer, and for a moment they merely moved together in awkward silence.

She was a good dancer, at least. He'd give her that. She didn't seem to be paying attention at all and yet she kept perfect time with her steps. And as she wasn't paying attention, he was free to study her.

She was a slight little thing, pale and thin and with hair so white-blonde, she might have been a spirit in his arms. Or maybe an angel.

There was that flare of pity again, unwelcome and out of place. It wasn't as though he could do something to help her evade her fate. Not even Rodrick could stop this marriage from happening, and Alex knew his friend was far from thrilled with the match.

But she didn't fight it, Rodrick had said. Alex remembered how frustrated Rodrick had been when he'd spoken of his sister's match. According to Rodrick, she'd gone along with the courtship quite willingly.

"When do you set off on your journey?" she asked.

"This very night," he said. It was a lie, but only a little one.

Her brows shot up. "Truly?"

"Mmm. Which is why I really must be off as soon as we're through here," he said.

He wasn't sure if he was enforcing this lie for his sake or

hers. He feared one more pitiful look from those pretty blue eyes and he'd do something utterly stupid. Like stay until the party ended to be her protector.

"Of course," she murmured.

"I hope to be at the first posting inn to change horses by sunrise," he lied. Because in for a penny, in for a pound, he supposed.

And truly, it was only a very minor lie. He *was* in a rush to head south where he would board a sailboat to Calais, though he didn't plan to leave until mid-morning.

"Where will you go?" she asked.

He blinked in surprise at the question. She seemed to actually care about his answer. "The usual places. France, Italy..." He shrugged. There were too many places to name.

Enough that he might never come back.

"Italy?" Her eyes widened wistfully.

He felt a smile tug at the corners of his lips at her dreamy expression. Unlike the smile she'd been wearing before, this wistful expression actually reached her eyes and made them soft. "You wish to go there, I take it?"

"I suppose." She smiled and he caught a sadness in her eyes. "Italy is where my sister currently resides, that's all. I would very much like to see her. To talk to her before..." She shook her head. "I just wish...I wish..."

She trailed off.

What do you wish? He found he rather desperately wanted to know.

Before Alex could question her, however, she smiled. The smile was blinding in its beauty, if slightly marred by wry cynicism that did not fit with the rest of her countenance. "But you know what they say, if wishes were horses."

He frowned. "I never heard that one."

"Oh. It's 'if wishes were horses, beggars would ride.'"

He nodded, absorbing the words. "That's...that's rather sad, actually."

He surprised himself with that statement, but there it was. That saying made his chest ache with bittersweet longing. Pity too.

What was it that she wished?

Her smile fell. "It is rather sad, isn't it?"

They went back to silence and a moment later he could have sworn he saw her transform right before his eyes.

"I am sorry you won't be here for the wedding," she said.

And she was back. The smiling simpleton. The woman who would make Lord Pickington a fine, vapid, beautiful broodmare.

He held back a sigh. "Yes. 'Tis a shame I'll miss it."

Another lie. This one much larger. He was outright elated to be missing the spectacle. He suspected she heard his lie for what it was because her lips pinched slightly. "Perhaps we'll meet again sometime."

"Perhaps."

But he hoped not. Even during this one short dance, Eloise had stirred emotions better left untouched. Long buried memories of his mother were threatening to rear up. Biddable and sweet, weak and frail...

Yes, he knew exactly what Eloise's life would look like from here on out, and it was pity that had him saying at last, "I hope we do meet again."

He was rewarded with a smile for the platitude that he was certain they both knew was a lie.

3

It was nice of him to lie.

That was all Eloise could think as she watched her brother's friend take his leave. He hadn't seemed to like her much, and that was fine. She hadn't particularly liked him either. He was much too blunt. And his gaze was nothing if not judgmental.

She suspected it would take much to earn that man's good opinion and marrying his uncle had ensured that she would not.

Which was fine. Because she didn't care for him either.

But Eloise wasn't terribly good at thinking ill of anyone— it didn't sit right. And so, she focused on the fact that, rude or not, judgmental or not...it had been nice of him to lie at the end of their dance.

Of course, he didn't wish to see her again, no more than she wished for another waltz with him.

But he'd been polite enough to lie to spare her feelings, and so she would think well of him, she decided as she flitted from one group to the next, trying and failing to calm her nerves.

But no amount of focusing her thoughts on her brother's unusual friend could steer her thoughts from what this party was for. No one would let her forget. Every group she joined felt the need to remark on the upcoming wedding as she hopped from one cluster to another.

Also, it was possible she was avoiding her fiancé.

Which was silly. They were to be married the next day. What did she hope to gain by evading his company this evening?

She didn't know, but her racing heart and trembling limbs seemed to have a mind of their own. They sent her scrambling in the opposite direction whenever she saw him heading her way, until she started to feel like a child playing a game of hide and seek.

She just needed a moment alone, that was all. If she could just have one second of solitude, a respite from this crush of well-wishers.

A darkened hallway beckoned, and she fled from the room, tugging at the lace edge of her chemisette as if that scrap of fabric was what impeded her breathing.

She found reprieve at last in Pickington's library. Soon to be *her* library.

Oh goodness, she truly could not get enough air.

Dark as it was, she still recognized the room and she moved forward until she hit the edge of an armchair and let herself sink against it.

"Ah, there you are." Pickington's voice in the doorway had her straightening with a strangled sound. "I was wondering where you'd run off to."

His voice was loud and sanctimonious in the quiet of the library. As if he were scolding her even as he asked, "Are you all right, my dear?"

My dear. The endearment felt wrong. There was no kindness in it, which made the words sound like mockery rather than affection.

"Yes," she managed, though her voice still held a breathless quality she despised. "I just needed a moment alone, that's all."

Please, let me have a moment. Please.

She bit her lip to keep from begging, as her gaze was held rapt by the sight of him in the doorway. Silhouetted as he was, it was almost possible to forget that he was three times older than her.

In fact, as he moved toward her, all she could notice was how much larger he was compared to her. She'd always been vaguely aware, of course. They'd stood side by side often enough. He'd even stooped down to kiss her cheek on more than one occasion.

But as he entered the darkened room, she was keenly aware of his height even more than his age.

His height...and his breath.

Her stomach churned. How was it possible that the stench of his breath could reach her from several feet away?

But then it wasn't several feet, it was two at best. And then one as he kept approaching.

"The guests will begin to wonder at your absence," he said.

"Y-yes, my apologies. I...I just wanted..."

"I think I know what you wanted, my dear," he said. The smugness of his tone made her stiffen.

"You do?"

"Of course. It's only natural for a girl your age to be curious." He moved closer still, and if it weren't for the armchair behind her, Eloise would have backed away.

As it was, there was nowhere for her to go. Her heart was slamming against her ribcage. She was trapped.

His hand came out and touched her face. "We'll be

married tomorrow. I suppose no one will mind if I have a taste tonight, eh?"

Her lips worked but no sound came out. A taste? A taste of what?

The feel of his lips against hers was so jarring—so, revolting—that she tore her head away with a cry.

"Don't be such a ninny," he growled. This time he grabbed the back of her head before leaning down to kiss her again.

She squirmed, trying to get away. It wasn't just panic now making her heart race, it was terror.

Horror.

His lips were hard and merciless, crushing hers as his fingers dug into her skull. The height and breadth of him made her feel like she was suffocating. Drowning.

She was trapped.

It was instinct that had her reaching out, sheer panic and fear that had her shoving him away.

"Why you little minx," he growled. The anger in his voice gave her a start.

He was angry with her?

"You think you can push me away, do you? As of tomorrow you are mine, girl."

"Tomorrow," she said, the word tasting of bile. "Not tonight." She looked past him toward the door. Candlelight flickered in the hallway and the sound of revelry reached her.

So close but still too far away.

"Everyone is out there," she said, desperation in her voice as he stalked closer again.

His laughter was cruel. "You think your parents don't know what we're doing in here right now? No one cares. We all know that I own you now."

I own you.

The words made her stomach plummet and her legs shake.

"Tomorrow's formalities just make it official."

"But we should wait until it is official," she said.

Even she could hear her pleading. Begging.

His laughter mocked her.

"Wait for what?" He moved so close that she could feel the brush of his jacket against her gown as he gripped her arms. "Might as well get this over with, eh? We need you with child right away. I've wasted too much time as it is."

Her mouth went dry as a scream threatened to escape.

She knew what he meant, of course. Her mother had given her and Charlotte a horrifyingly awkward speech on how a woman came to be with child when their engagements were announced.

But now the reality of what it meant hit her.

More than that, she heard it in his voice, the reality she'd never quite wanted to face. That this was all she was to him. A means to an heir.

Just as his status was all that mattered to her parents.

He was a means to a title.

He'd get her with child and then she'd have served her purpose. Or she wouldn't, and he'd find a way to replace her with someone who could.

Tears stung the back of her eyes as he gripped her arms so tightly she knew she'd see bruises. And then his mouth was back, reeking worse than ever, and hitting her square in the face as he crushed her to him.

No. No! This could not be her life. This could not be all she was meant for.

She'd never even enjoyed a ball. She'd never been courted. She'd never seen anything of the world like Charlotte or studied a topic that enamored her like Rodrick.

She'd never done anything, and as of tomorrow her fate would be sealed.

She dragged her mouth away from his as she gagged and struggled.

The future felt darker than this room, and she was trapped. Not just in his arms, but in life. Her life was ending in the morning.

This was what she had to look forward to.

And all at once, she couldn't bear it. The panicky sensation she'd been battling all night turned into something else entirely. Rage, maybe. Or determination.

She couldn't say because her mind went blank as her blood roared past her ears.

She shoved against Pickington with all her strength, and he must have been caught off guard because she wasn't *that* strong and he was so much larger...

And yet, he went flying backward, hitting an end table with a grunt before he fell onto the floor with a great thud.

Was he all right? She couldn't say. She couldn't see.

But her heart was fluttering like mad and she didn't stop to think.

She ran.

In the candlelit hall she looked left and right. To her right she could hear the party guests. Her family would be there, but...would they help her?

What would she say?

Perhaps Rodrick would, but her father? Her mother?

Tears stung her eyes as she faced the truth. They would not help her. They'd be horrified by what she'd done.

He might have acted out of line by assaulting her tonight, but as of tomorrow morning it would be his right. He could do with her whatever he wished.

He would punish her however he saw fit.

She choked on a sob as she panted, leaning forward to catch her breath.

Her parents would force her to apologize, and the

marriage would be on. And the next time he came at her like this, she would have no option but to obey.

The sound of Pickington's groan from the library behind her had her bursting into action. She ran to the left, toward the kitchens and the alleyway beyond.

From there where would she go?

She knew not.

All she knew was that when she stumbled out past the servants, who were too busy to pay her much mind, she found herself panting in the cold night air.

Steam plumed before her but at last she could finally breathe.

The door closed behind her with a snick, and relief flooded through her. Her legs kept moving as if she had somewhere to be until she found herself standing before a home two doors down from Pickington's.

It was then that reality returned and one thing became very, very clear.

This...was a bad plan.

No, it was worse than that. This was no plan at all.

Eloise stood there gaping before this home, which was not hers nor her fiancé's.

She had no plan.

None.

She wrapped her arms around herself as a whole new panic began to set in. This one had nothing to do with her future as Lady Pickington and everything to do with surviving the night.

She stared at Pickington's townhouse, which glowed bright against the dark night, each window offering a glimpse into the festivities inside.

Her family was in there.

That was where she ought to be.

The sounds from within could be heard from where she

stood just down the street, ignoring the curious look of a coach driver and its horse, both of whom seemed to be waiting to see what she was about to do.

What would she do?

Think, Eloise. What would Rodrick do?

But no, he was a man. The same rules did not apply.

What would Charlotte do? She'd hatch some sort of scheme. She'd use her brain and come up with something.

Eloise bunched her hands in her skirts as she shivered. One thing was certain, she could not just stand here and wait to be found.

Any minute now they'd be looking for her. Pickington would tell her parents what she'd done and they'd all come looking for her.

If she was lucky.

If Pickington chose to be cruel, he'd tell the entire crowd what she'd done and she'd be ruined by sunrise.

Sunrise. She found herself blinking at the horizon. The sun wasn't up yet, but the word alone jarred a memory.

I hope to be at the first posting inn to change horses by sunrise. Wasn't that what the viscount had said?

A flicker of...something had her turning away from Pickington's lively townhome. She knew where Lord Wycliffe lived. She'd dropped her brother there once on her way to the theater.

Her slippered feet picked up their pace even as a voice of reason bombarded her with questions. *Where are you going? What are you going to do?*

She did not know. But two things were clear. One, she could not stay out here in this cold. She'd freeze to death. Or worse. If any ne'er-do-wells were to come along...well, she shuddered to think of what might become of her.

So no, she could not stay here. But the second fact was equally clear.

She could not go back there.

This fact didn't even require consideration. Her parents would not understand, and even if Pickington were willing to forgive her...

She wasn't certain she wanted to be forgiven.

Without knowing what she meant to do when she got there, she followed her instincts and headed toward the viscount's home. He'd be gone so there was no danger that he would force her to return, but perhaps his housekeeper would let her stay warm by the fire while she decided what to do next.

Yes, it was the start of a plan, at least.

Albeit...not a very good one.

4

*D*espite the freeze that stung her toes and had her limbs trembling, Eloise found herself pausing to stare up at the brick townhome. It was far less ornate and on a side street that wasn't so fashionable as Pickington's. But something about Wycliffe's home was far more appealing than his uncle's.

Probably the fact that Pickington was not in residence.

That was obviously its biggest boon.

She'd circled the home twice, not quite able to bring herself to knock. But now she found herself standing by the side entrances where the servants and merchants came and went. Surely if she were to beseech the housekeeper, she ought to arrive at the kitchen door.

But what if the housekeeper wasn't awake?

And what if they turned her away?

And what if...

She shook her head and stomped her feet to bring back some feeling to her toes. *Really, Eloise, you've come this far. Might as well see this through.*

And if they said no, well then...

Well then she'd ask to borrow a coat, at the very least. Maybe someone would give her some boots. And then...

Oh heavens, she couldn't think about *and then*. She had no clue what would happen *and then*.

One task at a time. She had to at least try to find herself a place to spend the night, and when she was safe and warm, she'd think about what was to come next.

She knocked on the door.

No answer.

She knocked again.

Again, no answer.

A freezing cold wind whipped around her and set her teeth chattering. Later she'd say that was what made her do it, because that was the moment she tried the doorknob.

It opened.

So easily, really. She bit her lip as she struggled with what she was about to do. Not really whether or not she was going to do it—the wind had rather made up her mind on that one as well. More like, she was grappling to come to grips with it.

She'd never thought herself a burglar before.

Then, of course, she'd never suspected she'd be a runaway bride before either.

The thought had a squeaking noise escaping her throat, though whether it was a horrified shriek or a stifled hysterical giggle, she couldn't begin to say. It did startle her out of her reverie, though, and when the next gust of wind cut through her thin silk gown, she pushed the door open and stepped inside.

A fire crackled low in the hearth, and despite her trepidation, Eloise gave herself a moment to enjoy the newfound warmth.

Taking stock of the dark, empty kitchen around her, she sank onto a bench next to the fire as she asked herself *what's next?*

Should she give a shout? Find the servants' quarters and knock politely on a door?

She winced at the thought of the fright she might give some poor maid or footman.

Or perhaps... She eyed the dwindling fire with longing as another chill swept through her. Perhaps she could just stoke the fire a bit and stay warm through the night.

She'd likely have some sort of plan by morning so perhaps she'd be gone before anyone was the wiser.

Yes. That was the best idea of the lot. And if a voice screamed 'where will you go come morning?' she managed to ignore it quite completely. She focused instead on adding some kindling to the fire and warming her frozen fingers and toes.

It was amazing how one's priorities could shift when one was frozen to the core. She'd have to think about what came next eventually, but for a few moments, all that mattered was that she was warm and safe.

Well, relatively safe. So long as no one found her and alerted Pickington to her presence here.

She nibbled on her lip as her brows furrowed.

Think, Eloise. What would Charlotte do?

Charlotte. Her heart ached at the thought of her reckless sister. What would she say if she knew Eloise had done something even more reckless than she had?

Another hysterical giggle threatened and she clapped a hand over her mouth.

Charlotte wouldn't believe it. But she'd support her. Her younger sister would undoubtedly support her in leaving Pickington. Even if it meant ruin.

And at least Charlotte was already wed and Rodrick was happily engaged. Surely her own ruin wouldn't ruin them in turn...would it?

No, she didn't think it would.

Rodrick might not understand—or maybe he would, she did not know. He was a kind brother, but he, like Eloise, had been raised to be dutiful and to respect the responsibilities that came with their family's status.

So, he might feel for her, but would he truly understand?

She wasn't certain. But Charlotte definitely would. She'd always chafed under the obligations her parents thrust on her. So much so that her parents had sent Charlotte off to live with their eccentric great aunt.

Eloise found herself staring at the flickering flames intently as a new idea began to take form. It wasn't exactly a plan...more like a farfetched notion. But it was a start. It at least gave her something to think about.

A creak and a shuffling noise had her whirling about but when no one entered, she realized it was likely just the house settling and she drew in a deep, steadying breath.

She was alone, but not for long. At what hour did servants rise to start their chores?

She frowned. She was not certain, but she suspected it was before sunrise, which meant her time here was running out. She'd need to be on her way soon. Perhaps she ought to start by looking for a coat to borrow.

Steal, that blasted voice of reason pointed out. *You mean steal.*

No, it was merely borrowing. She'd find some way to return it to its rightful owner once she got where she was going.

And where is that?

She stood abruptly. Decisions needed to be made, and it was time to face the fact that there was no easy road in sight.

A new resolve straightened her spine and she held her hands out over the fire as if she could absorb enough heat to keep her warm on this next leg of her journey.

Your journey where? Think, Eloise. A plan is in order...even if it's not a particularly good one.

Any plan was better than no plan.

With another deep breath, she mentally reviewed what she knew to be true.

She could not go back home.

She was not certain she could trust her parents to shield her from Pickington or his wrath. Even if Rodrick would, so long as her parents or Pickington knew where she was and had her in their sights, she would not be safe.

Charlotte and her great aunt were the only ones who might understand. And they were both in Italy at the moment.

"Which means I am going to Italy," she told the fire.

The fire was unimpressed. But saying it aloud gave Eloise another burst of courage. She could do this. People traveled all the time, every day of the year.

Perhaps not young unchaperoned ladies, but she would find a way. All she needed was...

Everything, really.

A coach to take her south to board a ship across the channel. Fare for said ship. And then some means of traveling the continent...

Her legs wobbled as fear set in.

All right, perhaps this would be more difficult than she'd first thought. But really, everything she'd just listed could be attained with the right amount of money.

Surely she could hire a chaperone, and pay someone to guide her, and...

Yes. With enough coin, she could overcome any obstacle.

"Right," she told the fire. "So now I just need money."

The fire crackled in response. But she heard her answer clearly enough. She was in a wealthy man's home. A gentleman's house and the gentleman was not in attendance.

She turned to face the kitchen, her breath quickening.

Could she do it? It was one thing to burgle a near-empty house. But to steal?

Nay, borrow.

Charlotte or her aunt would help her to pay Wycliffe back whatever she stole.

Took.

Borrowed.

Oh bother.

She'd deal with the semantics and the guilt some other time. Right now, time was of the essence. If she truly were to do this, she had to act now and be gone before any servants woke to find her.

"Right. We are doing this," Eloise said softly. "Now, where would Wycliffe keep his coin?"

Dread rippled through her as she crept through the kitchen to the hallway beyond. Fears allayed her at every turn.

What if he'd taken all his money with him? Did gentlemen do that? Or perhaps he kept it in a bank. What if he didn't trust his servants and so—

She shook her head with an exasperated sigh as she reached the dark, thickly carpeted hallway that led to the main portion of the house.

There was only one way to find out if he had money in this house and that was to look for it. Her palms were clammy with nerves as she felt her way along the hall. A candle would be nice right about now. But at least there was some moonlight coming through the windows near the front of the house.

She opened one door to her left and found a closet. Shutting it, she hurried along. The next room looked far more promising. Judging by the large desk in the center of his room, this was Wycliffe's study. "As good a place to start as any," she whispered.

There was no fire, but there were windows. The curtains were closed but for a small gap so she hurried over and threw them open.

"There, that's better," she whispered.

She knew she ought to be totally silent, but the sound of her own voice helped to alleviate some of her fears.

It did not escape her that she ought not to be the frightened one. She was the thief here, after all. Surely the servants, if they were to wake, would be startled by her.

So there.

She was devious and cunning, and she tried her best to truly believe that.

"If I were coins, where would I be?" she asked the room at large. "Right. I'll start with the desk."

She pulled open the top drawer but merely found writing utensils and some parchment. The second was even less fruitful. As she went through the absurd amount of drawers, she tried to keep her nerves at bay by tallying how much she'd need.

She told herself she wouldn't take any more than that.

Because she was not a thief. Merely a borrower.

She was on the bottom-most drawer when a movement out of the corner of her eye had her bolting upright with a startled cry.

A little ball sped right toward her before a soft bundle of fur pressed against her skirts.

"Oh my goodness!" She clapped a hand over her mouth as she gasped, her heart rocketing into her throat. The ball of fuzz was nuzzling her shins and snuffling at her feet.

A dog.

She let out a relieved breath as her heart recovered from the shock.

She bent down to pet the adorable little creature. "Little dear," she crooned softly. "You gave me quite the start."

"How amusing..." The deep voice behind her was utterly without humor despite what he said. "I was just about to say the same to you."

Eloise let out a startled squeak as she whirled about to face the man in the doorway. Another strangled screech escaped at the sight of his pistol...aimed straight at her bosom.

5

A woman.

It was a blasted *woman* rifling through his drawers in the middle of the night.

Alex peered into the darkness, but all he could see was a female silhouette against the moonlit window behind her. Her voice had been little more than a whisper, but one thing was clear. "You're not one of the servants."

"No."

That was it. No other explanation forthcoming. Though what sort of explanation he'd expected he couldn't have said.

But at least he didn't have to sack one of his employees before leaving the country.

So, there was that.

His pistol weighed heavily in his hands as silence filled the darkened room. And all at once he felt like a cad aiming a weapon at a lady in his home. He dropped it to his side as he headed toward the desk.

The lady in question scurried out of his way as if he were coming to strike her. "Don't try to run," he said, his voice gruff as he caught a whiff of a delicate scent reminiscent of oranges and vanilla.

It was light and sweet and...oddly familiar. It was also not at all what he'd expect from a robber.

He found the matches and candle easily enough as they were where he'd last left them. The strike of the match made the woman beside him give a start, and she was backing away from him again as he held it aloft.

Not that she had anywhere to go. He stood between her and the only exit.

"Now, let's have a look at you," he said.

"I-I'd rather you didn't," she said softly.

No, *politely*. Her tone was as even and mild as if they were taking tea in the parlor.

That mild tone, the soft, lilting voice...

He had an image of a weak, breathless female in his arms from earlier that night.

No.

It couldn't be.

He stepped forward and lifted the candle...

It was.

"Eloise?" The name broke from him with a start and she cringed as if he'd shouted.

"It's Miss Haverford," she said primly, smoothing her hands over her skirts while her gaze fixed on the rug at her feet as if this particular pattern was of great interest to her.

"Miss Haverford," he echoed, chastened like a schoolboy for having had the gall to break from decorum and use her given name at a time like this.

He cleared his throat, amusement and horror battling it out now that shock was waning.

He shouldn't be amused. This was *not* amusing. Why, if they were discovered together...

If anyone knew that she was here, in his home...alone.

Horror won the battle handily.

"Eloise, what are you doing here?"

She cleared her throat, her chin lifting, though her gaze wouldn't budge from his blasted carpet. "I did not expect you to be at home."

"No. Clearly."

Silence.

As she was hardly forthcoming with an explanation, his addled brain tried to come up with one for her.

It came up blank for a frighteningly long moment. But truly...

Miss Eloise Haverford. Diamond of the first water. Belle of the blasted ball. The guest of honor at tonight's celebration. His uncle's bride-to-be. And...oh curse it all. The sister of one of his closest friends.

Which meant, of course...she was his responsibility.

Alex drew in a deep breath and pinched the bridge of his nose. He'd been tossing and turning in bed when he'd heard someone moving about belowstairs. He should have just let it be.

Perhaps the girl would have found what she was after and been gone by the time he woke. But what was she after? And gone where? She had a wedding to attend in the afternoon. He knew that as well as anyone.

The blasted invitation was sitting on the desk not two feet away.

"What are you doing here?" he asked again. Because clearly, he needed help. He considered himself a quick fellow, but he couldn't begin to reason why Miss Eloise Haverford was in his study, of all places.

She shifted, her hands clasping and unclasping as she worried her lower lip. Somehow this small gesture made him feel like the worst sort of heel.

"Were you...sleepwalking?" he guessed.

It sounded ridiculous the moment it slipped out, but at least it surprised her enough that her gaze lifted to meet his, her brows arching. "Pardon?"

He shrugged helplessly. "Help me out here, Eloise. I've just woken to find my best friend's gently bred, soon-to-be married, tediously proper little sister rifling through my study. I thought sleepwalking might be the most charitable excuse."

"Oh." She winced.

And he had the most unusual suspicion that he could read her thoughts. And what she was thinking seemed to be something along the lines of, *Drat. I wish I would have thought of that.*

"You're not a spy, are you?" he tried again, this time not without a hint of humor. Because blast it all, despite the horror of what would happen if they were to be caught alone together, there was something hilariously ludicrous about this entire situation.

"Of course not," she said with an indignant huff. Then her head tipped to the side. "Why? Do you have secrets the crown would like to discover?"

He laughed, the sound shocking both of them, it seemed.

"All right, then," he said. "Why don't you tell me why you are *not* at your fiancé's home or safely tucked in bed getting some rest before your big day tomorrow?"

Even in the candlelight, he saw her go pale. All blood and life seemed to seep from her pretty face.

He also saw her shiver.

Curse it. "You're freezing."

"No, it's just...well, yes. A bit. It was a rather chilly walk over here, I'm afraid."

He stared at her dumbstruck for a long moment. Did she have any idea how odd she sounded, speaking for all the world like this was some social occasion. As if these were calling hours and she was here with her brother's supervision.

He gave his head a shake. "Fine. To the parlor," he said with a curt wave of his arm. "There's a fire still going in there."

"Oh, thank you, my lord," she said as he led the way to the parlor.

"Might as well be comfortable for this visit," he grumbled.

"Well, yes, about that..." she started.

She didn't finish.

He glanced back. Her hands fluttered at her sides as if she could summon words or perhaps perform a pantomime to explain it all away.

When they reached the parlor, he busied himself by lighting more candles and stoking the fire.

She stood just beside him, and she seemed slighter than ever as she wrapped her arms around herself with a shiver, her lips trembling as she stared down into the flames.

"Do you need food?" he asked.

"No, thank you."

Good. Because he had no idea where anything was in his kitchen, and he didn't suppose adding his nosey housekeeper and her opinions to this tableau would help matters.

"Er...have a seat." He pulled one of the chairs closer to the fire for her with a jerky movement.

Lud, when had he become so unbearably awkward?

He supposed late night visits from innocent young ladies had this effect on him. Now he knew. In the event this ever happened again, he'd be prepared with the proper etiquette. He'd offer warmth and food straight away the next time a silly young debutante broke into his home.

She sank into the seat gracefully, spreading her skirts out to dry.

Because they were wet. Because...

"You walked here," he said, stating the obvious. "Alone."

She flinched but didn't deny it. He raked a hand through his hair as a surge of terror hit him square in the chest. In the course of one heartbeat his mind came up with a hundred different ways she might have been harmed on that short walk.

The thought of her hurt or mishandled or...worse.

Unacceptable.

"Have you lost your mind?" he stared down at her as she dipped her head, recoiling from his wrath. "Do you have any idea what might have happened?"

She didn't answer.

When she finally spoke, she seemed determined to act as though they were at Almack's and not alone in his parlor in the dead of night. "I did not intend to disturb your sleep, Lord Wycliffe. If you'll just allow me to stay until daylight, I will be on my way."

"On your way...where? Home?" He looked around him for the jacket he'd discarded earlier. Too late he realized he'd been entertaining this young lady while wearing nothing but his breeches and shirt. "I'll escort you there now."

"No!" She jumped up from her seat. "I mean...no. Please." She winced slightly. "And thank you."

He shook his head. "So polite, even when you've gone mad."

Her lips curved down in a frown. "I haven't gone mad."

"Haven't you? Then tell me what you are doing here."

She clamped her mouth shut, but the look in her eyes...

Blast it all, she looked stunning.

Not the sort of thing he should be noticing right now, but it was impossible not to. She was always pretty. Too pretty, in fact. He'd never liked her sort of pretty. She had that perfect doll-like quality to her that most men adored and he abhorred. It was so...so...delicate.

So dainty.

So...*good*.

And there was nothing that repulsed him more than an obedient, docile young lady with no mind of her own.

But this here now...that spark in her eyes when she glared up at him in silent defiance...

The air caught in his lungs and it seemed like it meant to stay there forever as his heart gave a loud slam against his ribcage.

That spark of fury made her...not pretty. Glorious. She was a righteous, avenging angel sent down to smite mere mortals like him.

The ridiculous thought was gone with the blink of an eye as he ordered himself to focus. But he wasn't sure he'd ever entirely rid himself of the image.

She sank back into her seat, her gaze turning wary. "Why are you staring at me like that?"

With a sigh, he squatted down beside her so his face was level with hers. "Look here, Eloise—"

"Miss Haverford," she corrected.

"Until a few hours from now," he amended.

She blanched. He knew he wasn't imagining it when her face went sickly pale and her eyes filled with a terror that made his own gut clench with sympathy.

"You're running away," he said. It wasn't a question.

"I am not," she spit like a little devil.

An entirely inappropriate smile tugged at his lips but he fought it as he met her gaze evenly. "Miss Haverford..."

"Yes?"

"Are you running away from your wedding?"

"I am not...*not* running away," she said slowly.

And he watched as horror filled her eyes along with...oh no.

"Do not cry," he ordered harshly.

She sniffed. "I am not crying."

"Indeed. Just as you are not *not* running away."

She winced at hearing her own weak response thrown back at her. "Oh all right, I am running away. But you make it sound so...cowardly."

His chin jerked back at the force in her tone. "Isn't it?"

She pressed her lips together and that anger was back, making her eyes glow and her entire being come alive, crackling with energy just as surely as the fire snapped and flared.

And then it died just as quickly as it surfaced.

"Maybe," she said with a delicate little shrug. "I do not know."

The fire crackled noisily beside them as he considered her. "Your family will be worried."

She didn't answer.

"Your fiancé will be concerned," he tried again.

Her jaw clenched and her lips worked. "I will not marry him," she finally spit out.

"I see." He couldn't blame her. In fact, he felt a surge of respect for this girl that he never would have expected. "Does he know that?"

"Uh..." She winced, and the emotions that flickered over her face made him tense.

"Eloise?"

She whipped her head around. "It is Miss Haverford," she snapped. "And what are you doing here?"

His brows arched and he swallowed a laugh just in time. "This is my home, if you'll recall."

"Yes, but you were supposed to be gone." Her brows drew together.

A fierce, courageous...adorable little warrior.

"Was I?" Oh yes, it was taking everything in him not to laugh just now.

Her lips pursed and her eyes narrowed as she turned in

her seat to face him directly. "You told me while we were dancing that you would be gone before first light. You said you were leaving straight away."

"Did I say that?" he mused.

Her brows drew down farther.

He shrugged. "I was trying to be polite."

"Polite?"

"Yes, it seemed kinder to say I had to depart immediately than to admit that your party and the guests assembled made me want to tear my hair out with their tedious small talk."

Her lips parted in surprise.

"However," he continued. "If I had known that my being gracious gave you the impression that you could help yourself to my home and my coin...trust me when I say I shall cease being polite henceforth."

Her eyes and mouth widened and he saw the protest forming—before she realized that he was teasing. And then she burst out in a laugh that was loud and sweet and genuine...

And perhaps just a touch hysterical.

She clapped a hand over her mouth, her eyes widening even further with horror. "Oh good heavens," she breathed from behind her fingers. "What have I done?"

6

Sanity was such a fickle creature. One moment Eloise was certain she had a grasp of her new reality and the situation wherein she'd found herself. The next, she found herself gaping at a near stranger trying not to weep uncontrollably.

He clearly saw her battle, because the poor man looked horrified. "Please don't cry. Please, Eloise, I'm begging you."

She blinked a few times rapidly, but that just made the welling tears spill over. She swiped at them with the back of her gloved hand. "I'm sorry," she muttered. "I'm trying not to."

They sat like that for a long moment, her swiping at tears and sniffling, trying her best to quell this wave of emotion. And he resting on his haunches as he regarded her warily, like she was some rabid, feral beast.

"They're just tears, Lord Wycliffe," she finally said, not without a hint of exasperation. "They are not contagious."

She was gratified to see his lips twitch with mirth.

He did that a lot, she'd noticed. Even when he was shocked and horrified and rightfully befuddled, there were these glimpses of amusement that he couldn't seem to help. His lips twitched with it and it danced in his eyes.

Funny, only earlier tonight she'd thought him to be so unbearably grim. And there was still a cynical tinge to his amusement. He wasn't exactly jovial, that much was certain. But that hint of humor did wonders to soften his harsh edges.

After a while, he scratched the back of his head and gave her a rueful grimace. "Do you, uh...do you want to tell me about your, uh...your feelings?"

Her answering scoff was hardly polite, and not in the least ladylike. Did she wish to air her feelings to a man so clearly horrified by any displays of emotion? "No, thank you."

His shoulders sank with relief and he came to stand. "Right. Then I suppose the best course of action would be for me to send for your brother—"

"No!" She shot up as well. "No, please, Lord Wycliffe—"

"Alex," he said.

"What?"

He smiled and her heart took a giant leap in her chest. "I'd like to think that tonight's events have made us closer, don't you think?"

She pressed her lips together. He was teasing her again. He expected her to protest at the intimacy as she had been every time he'd called her Eloise.

With a wave of embarrassment she realized how silly she must look to him. Trying to maintain some dignity while having been caught red-handed. "Alex, then," she said softly, dipping her head to regain her composure. "Please, please don't send for my brother. Or my parents." She glanced up with blatant pleading. "And please don't tell Lord Pickington I'm here."

She hated the flicker of pity in his eyes even as she was grateful for it.

If he took pity on her, then he might help her.

"Eloise," he started slowly.

"I was looking for money," she said.

He blinked. "Yes, I gathered as much. For what?"

"You were right," she said. "I was running away. If I can get to my aunt and my sister, they will take me in. I know it."

He eyed her for a long moment, his gaze serious but unreadable. "You will be ruined, you know that, yes?"

She swallowed down a terse retort. *Of course I will be ruined. I am not so very dimwitted as all that.* Instead, she said, "I already am."

He winced. "Not if we get you back before anyone notices."

She arched her brows and glanced meaningfully toward the window where sunrise was already starting to lighten the horizon. When she looked back, she was almost certain she could see his brain scrambling to come up with some sort of solution.

"I'll take you home," he said. "To *your* home. You can tell your parents that you'd fallen ill and—"

"No."

He arched his brows. "No?"

She shook her head. "No."

Her mind's eye filled with the image of Pickington's mouth on hers and she shuddered with revulsion. "I cannot marry him. I will not." She wet her lips as another memory surfaced—Pickington falling to the ground after she'd shoved him away. "I've already told Pickington as much."

In a manner of speaking.

"I see," he said.

He clearly did not see. Not the entirety of the situation, at least.

"I cannot go back there," she said. "Not to him and not to my parents. He'll have told them what I did."

His brows came down, and the concern in his eyes made her chest ache and her eyes water all over again.

"What about Rodrick?" he said. "He'll help you."

"Perhaps, but then I would be asking him to side against my parents," she said. "And that is not fair."

He seemed surprised that she'd thought this through. As if she could do anything but think through the ramifications of her rash actions.

"But then..." She swallowed hard. "It is also not fair of me to put you in such a terrible position..."

"No, no," he said, his tone dry as he waved aside her comment. "We've already established that I am at fault for so rudely being at home when I was supposed to be out."

She pressed her lips together. She would not laugh.

This was most definitely not a laughing matter.

"I do have to leave though, Eloise."

The gentleness of his tone struck her.

He held his hands out, palms up in a helpless gesture. "My trunk is already stowed on the carriage and the horses are ready... I wasn't lying entirely, you see."

"Yes, I see," she murmured.

He needed to be gone, and he needed her out of his hair to do so.

And just like that she was hit with reality all over again. Oh, what had she *done*?

She squeezed her eyes tight. "If you could just lend me some money, I am certain I can make my way—"

"Alone? I don't think so." He seemed so affronted, for a moment she forgot he was a dashing rake because he sounded for all the world like a fretful old spinster.

"Why not? You're about to travel alone." She straightened, hope flickering so suddenly she gasped.

"No." His tone was hard and flat.

Her insides fell just as quickly as they'd risen. "But—"

"No," he said again, stronger this time. "I am not escorting a runaway bride to the continent...no matter how much I might pity her."

She scowled. "I did not ask for your pity."

"But you have it all the same," he said, not unkindly. They were facing one another fully now, and this close she could see the stubble on his chin and the dark circles beneath his eyes.

She was keeping him from what little sleep he could have before setting out on this adventure.

She ought to feel guilty, she supposed, but instead all she felt was...resentment. How easy it was for him. An eligible young viscount with no lack of fortune or freedom. Certainly he might be expected to marry one day, but no one could force him.

And until that day, he had all the freedom in the world.

Never in her life had Eloise felt sorry for herself—she knew quite well that she was lucky. She'd been born to wealth and class and with attractive looks and good health.

But at this particular moment, she was so envious she could spit.

And all because he was male. How different her life would be if she had been born a boy.

"Eloise, you must think this through." Alex's tone did nothing to assuage her irritation. He was talking to her like a child. As if she hadn't been thinking at all this entire evening.

Well, fine. She hadn't given it much thought when she'd pushed Pickington to the ground and run. But that was only because instinct had kicked in, and there'd been no time to sit and ruminate.

"I am thinking," she said through gritted teeth. "And while I understand why you might hesitate to escort me—"

"You understand, do you?" His brows arched and anger flashed in them. "Eloise, I feel sorry for your situation, I truly do. But if we were caught together, I'd be forced to marry you."

She blinked, trying to hide the fact that his words were a hard slap in the face.

He seemed to realize how that sounded because he quickly added, "And *you* would be forced to marry *me*."

"It wouldn't come to that," she said. "No one who knows us would see us together, and as soon as we got to the continent, you could leave me to go my own way and—"

"No, Eloise. Just...no."

All she could hear was her own breathing for a moment as they considered one another.

She wouldn't beg. "Will you at least lend me money so I might make my own way? I promise to pay you back if—"

"Eloise, think of your family."

"I am thinking of my family," she said. Her hands clenched at her sides. "I'm thinking of my parents, who care more about me becoming a countess than they do my happiness. I'm thinking that my life will be over the moment I wed that man. I'm thinking that all he or my parents see me as is a means to an end—"

"Eloise, I understand." His voice was unbearably gentle, his gaze terribly kind and horribly pitiful.

"No, you do not understand," she said. "Not really. Because you were not raised to merely agree and obey."

His jaw hardened suddenly. "You have no idea how I was raised."

She was temporarily stunned into silence. The humor in his eyes was gone in a flash and once more he was the autocratic, disdainful gentleman she'd first met. "I do sympathize with your plight," he said quietly, but with a coldness that made her shiver. "But this is not my problem. *You* are not my problem."

"But—"

A sharp rapping at the front door cut her protest short and she found herself sharing a wide-eyed look of shock with Alex.

He recovered first, holding up a warning finger. "Wait here." He started to walk toward the entranceway. "Do not move."

She didn't obey.

She didn't run away again—where would she go? But she did move so she was hidden behind the parlor door just in case the visitor came inside.

Who on earth could be coming to Alex's door at this hour?

She didn't have to wait long for her answer.

She heard the door thrown open, and Alex's exclamation. "Rodrick! What are you doing here?"

7

*A*lex was not a man given to bouts of fear.

He liked to think himself a brave man, for the most part. But the sight of one of his closest friends in his doorway had his insides clenching in horror.

The ramifications of Eloise being in his parlor hit him with full force.

"Alex, sorry to wake you..." Rodrick trailed off with a frown as he took in Alex's alert state. *"Did I wake you?"*

"No, I, uh...no." Alex ran a hand through his no doubt disheveled hair as he tried to collect himself. "What brings you here at this hour?"

Please do not say Eloise.

"Eloise," Rodrick said with a deep frown. "My sister..."

Alex's head swam with the improbability of it all. How did he know she'd come here? Was his home the most obvious place for a runaway bride to run off to and he was the last to know?

"She's missing," Rodrick ended.

Alex sighed with relief. So, he did not know she was there.

Rodrick's frown turned to one of confusion—likely because Alex had just sighed with relief.

Alex mustered an unconvincing, "That's horrible."

But at least Rodrick didn't know she was here. But wait...was that good or bad? Perhaps he should just tell Rodrick and hand Eloise over.

Yes, that was precisely what he ought to do.

Guilt nagged at him but he held the door open further all the same. "I think you ought to come inside."

"I really have no time to lose," Rodrick said, but even as he spoke, he followed Alex into the dark entranceway and into the parlor where...Eloise was not to be found.

Alex turned in a circle twice before he caught her hiding behind the door. And then, when he ought to have called her out, he found himself speechless.

She was staring at him with such wide eyes. Eyes filled with such pleading and hope and...trust.

There was trust there, like she expected him to do right by her.

He muttered an oath.

"I know it's quite late," Rodrick said. "And of course you have a journey ahead of you in the morning, but—"

"No, of course you should have come here," Alex said, turning back to find Rodrick hovering in the doorway.

Worry creased his friend's brow and Alex was struck by guilt all over again...but this time toward Rodrick.

Blast. The Haverford family was making him feel torn in two. To whom was he most obligated? The pitiful runaway bride or the concerned older brother...who also happened to be his friend?

He scratched the stubble on his jaw.

All of those philosophy and ethics classes he'd taken at school proved utterly useless in the face of this dilemma.

"It's just...I don't want this getting out," Rodrick said, fidgeting with the hat he held in his hand.

"Of course."

"I don't know where she could have gone," he continued as he paced the room.

Eloise's expression was pained as she watched her brother from her hiding spot.

Perhaps if Alex let Rodrick fret long enough, Eloise would give herself up. It had to be hard on her watching her brother worry so.

Hoping to help matters along, Alex asked, "Are your parents concerned?"

Rodrick scoffed, Eloise winced, and Alex immediately regretted the question.

"They're furious," he said. "They believe she got cold feet and ran. But Eloise would never do such a thing. Charlotte, yes, but Eloise? Never." He stopped pacing so close to the open door that Alex could see both siblings from his perspective.

If Rodrick just turned around he'd see her himself.

"I'm truly worried, Alex," he said. "I don't wish to make it publicly known that she's gone, but I knew I could trust you and the others to help me search for her."

"Of course." His throat felt far too tight. If he were wearing a cravat he'd be tugging it off right about now.

He was a wretched friend.

Rodrick half turned, and Alex held his breath. But Rodrick didn't spot his sister and he turned back quickly, his brow creased with worry. "Alex, there's something else you should know..."

"What is it?" Alex asked when Rodrick trailed off. What he truly meant was, *what now?*

Alex was far from a feeble man, but this day was beginning to wear on him. He wasn't sure he could take many more surprises.

"It's why I came here first," Rodrick said, looking down at his feet. "I wanted you to hear all this from me before it became public knowledge. He is your uncle after all..."

Alex arched a brow, keenly aware of Eloise's gaze on him from just behind Rodrick. "That your sister stood him up for his own wedding? Can't say that I'm overly distressed, Rodrick, but I appreciate your concern."

But Rodrick still looked pained and wary.

"You know I don't have any affection for that old cad," he added, trying to ease Rodrick's concern. "I just wish I could see his face when he realizes your sister thwarted his plans."

He expected at least a huff of amusement from Rodrick. What he got was a sad sigh...and a glare from Eloise.

What was that for? Just because he was making light of her abandoning her fiancé? Didn't seem fair that he couldn't make a joke about it.

"He died, Alex," Rodrick said, and Alex's attention came back to Rodrick with a start.

He heard Eloise's gasp but either Rodrick didn't hear it or he'd thought it was a noise from the fire because he didn't turn around.

"He...what?" Alex asked.

Rodrick strode toward him. "That's why I came here first. I would like your help searching for Eloise, if you have some time to spare before you must leave on your journey—"

"Of course," Alex muttered, but his attention was fixed on Eloise.

Eloise, who looked beyond shocked by this news. She looked...shattered.

Curse it.

His insides twisted and fell at the sight of her pain, and it took everything in him not to push Rodrick aside and rush to her.

She hadn't loved the old man—heck, she'd run away from him. But he had been her fiancé and she seemed to be shaken to the core by the news of his death.

Alex ran a hand through his hair. *Don't cry.* He was all but shouting at her in his head. He couldn't bear to see her cry again. It had addled his brain and turned his insides to mush the first time around.

And now he was supposed to be coherent.

Rodrick was chattering away about the suddenness of his passing, and how Eloise had gone missing in the midst of it all. "My parents are using this to cover for her, of course. They've spread the word that she's grieving and cannot be consoled," he said, his tone bitter and irritated. "They care more about how this looks than her safety."

Alex nodded, hoping he wore the appropriate expression, but truly, he was too worried about Eloise's safety at the moment to pretend.

She was swaying now, her face white as a ghost in the shadows and her hands visibly shaking.

Surely, he couldn't hand her over to Rodrick when she was like this. Even if Rodrick believed him that this was innocent, Alex couldn't betray her like that. Not now when she was all vulnerable and helpless.

"We'd best be going," Alex said, shoving Rodrick toward the door.

"Yes, yes, of course," Rodrick said, stumbling as Alex gave him another strong push toward the door.

"Not a moment to lose," Alex continued. They were at the front door and out of Eloise's earshot when he finally thought to ask, "What happened to him?"

"Your uncle? The doctor seemed to think it was his heart."

Alex nodded. That made sense. His uncle had suffered heart issues in the past. "Not a surprise, I suppose."

"What matters now is finding—"

Thud.

It sounded like a sack of potatoes hitting the ground in the parlor, and Alex's heart clenched in response.

She'd fainted.

"What was that?" Rodrick asked, craning his neck.

"Nothing." And then. "The dog."

Rodrick pointed at Otis who was currently rubbing up against Alex's ankles. "That dog?"

"Another dog. A new one." He gave Rodrick another shove and started to close the door as he said, "Go fetch the others and I'll meet up with you at my uncle's. We can start the search from there."

He didn't wait for a response, shutting the door with a slam before running back to the parlor to find... "Eloise."

She was strewn out on the ground, unconscious. He knelt beside her, pleased when her eyelids fluttered and her chest rose and fell with even breaths.

That sight had him letting out the breath he'd been holding. She'd fainted, that was all. The poor girl had suffered one too many excitements for the day, apparently.

Not that he could blame her. It wasn't every day one ran away *and* discovered one's fiancé was dead. But still...

"Why didn't I hand you over to Rodrick when I had the chance?" he grumbled her as he bent down and wedged his arms beneath her shoulders and knees.

She was light as a feather in his arms, even with the full skirts of the gown. Her head lolled dangerously until he was upright and could shift her into what he hoped was a comfortable position.

And then he stood there for a moment because... "Now what?"

His housekeeper would be awake soon, along with the rest of the servants. And he had a ship to catch and a continent to tour.

He eyed the settee but wasn't entirely certain he wanted any passing servant to see her should they be up early. In the end, he settled for his bedroom.

Highly improper, but at this point propriety was well and truly out the window.

She began to stir when he was halfway up the stairs.

"Where...what..." Her eyes popped open and he saw her return to her senses with a jolt.

She physically jolted as well, and nearly upended them both with the sudden shift of weight in his arms. "What are you doing?"

"I was attempting to get you to bed."

Well, blast.

That hadn't come out right at all.

Her eyes widened with horror. "Pardon?"

"You fainted," he said, trying again. "I was merely trying to..."

He made the mistake of looking down at the lady in his arms. It was a very big mistake. This close he could see every shade of blue in her clear eyes, and now he knew that her lips were pink and fuller than he'd realized.

Not that he'd been taking note.

But now it was impossible not to take note. She was so close he could feel the warmth of her breath on his cheek and feel the silky softness of her hair against his neck.

He gritted his teeth. He'd been carrying her to bed out of chivalry, but now he knew for certain that chivalry was not his forte.

"Please put me down," she said, her tone pert and prim.

"We're almost there," he said. "I don't want you collapsing

on the stairs. This night has been bad enough without you suffering a head injury."

For reasons he couldn't begin to fathom, this comment made her blanch so thoroughly he was certain she would faint again.

She didn't. But she did make a soft squeaking noise which was just as alarming.

"Please, Eloise," he said, a hint of desperation in his tone. "Try to collect yourself until I've gotten you settled."

"I don't need to collect myself. I am fine."

"You fainted."

"I did not faint. I never faint."

Despite everything, there it was again. The swell of laughter. Mercy, but she'd be great fun to tease...

If she were not Rodrick's sister. Or meant to marry his now-dead uncle. Or on the run.

And preferably not alone in his house in the middle of the night.

He managed to keep the laughter out of his voice. "You do not faint, you say?"

"No." She stiffened in his arms as they reached the top of the staircase, a frown tugging at her lips. "I'm not prone to...to swooning."

"I see," he said as he entered his room and set her down atop the covers. "I shall be sure to tell the floor as much."

She blinked up at him.

"I believe there's a dent there where you landed."

8

*E*loise glared, her hands clenched into fists.

She did not swoon. She never fainted.

He smirked down at her.

"I did not swoon," she bit out.

Of all the stands to take, she understood completely that this was a silly one. But she was tired of being laughed at, and it was far easier to manage a swell of self-righteous irritation than to dwell on all that Rodrick had said.

Because if she let herself think about that...

Her belly twisted dangerously and she felt large, firm hands on her shoulders, holding her steady. "Easy there, love, or you might *not* faint again."

She blinked up at him. Oh, how could he be making jokes at a time like this?

"Pickington is dead," she said.

The hint of laughter in his eyes faded fast, his mouth falling into a flat line. "Yes. I'm sorry."

Her mouth gaped. *He* was sorry?

She was the one who had murdered the man.

Clapping a hand over her mouth she gave her head a shake. Maybe it wasn't her...

Her mind called up the memory. A hard shove, the way he'd thumped against something hard. Why hadn't she stopped to check on him? How long had he suffered?

Maybe...maybe it wasn't her blow that had killed him. How exactly *had* he died? Rodrick didn't say.

"If it helps at all, your brother said that his death was sudden. It was quick and no one could have seen this coming..."

She stared at Alex as his words registered. Any hope she might have held that he'd succumbed to some illness she'd been heretofore unaware of flittered away with his every word.

The death was sudden and unexpected.

Really, Eloise? What else could it be but the blow to the head he took at your hands?

Eloise made a noise somewhere between a gasp and a sob.

Alex knelt down and took her hands in his. "I don't mean to sound callous, Eloise. Clearly you harbor more affection for the man than I do...er, did..."

She stared at him in confusion. What was he on about?

He thought she held affection for Pickington?

No, she'd never had affection for Pickington. But that was the point, wasn't it?

She'd despised him so much, she'd murdered him.

A pathetic whimper escaped her and Alex winced.

She was beginning to see a pattern with this man. One thing was clear, he was not overly fond of displays of emotion. She suspected most men weren't, but he seemed to be thoroughly discomfited by them.

"I'm sorry," she said.

Even she wasn't quite sure what she was apologizing for. Being emotional? Breaking into his home? Killing his uncle?

He could take his pick, she supposed.

"Yes, well..." He came to stand, his tone brusque. "I don't have long to dally. Your brother is waiting for me." He arched a brow. "To find you."

She winced as the verbal blow landed.

Alex's gaze grew alarmingly intense. "He was worried, you know."

"Yes, I know." Her voice came out sounding more tart than she'd intended. Truly, tart was new for her, but tonight was a night of firsts.

He folded his arms. With him standing and glowering down at her like this, she felt like a child.

She was *not* a child.

"Thank you," she said, ducking her head to avoid his judgmental glare. "For not telling my brother I was here."

He sighed. "I didn't tell him, but I will if you do not return home, Eloise."

Her head came up with a snap. "What? Why?"

"Because Pickington is dead," he said, his voice loud and filled with impatience.

She flinched, which made him sigh again with ill-disguised exasperation.

"I hate to be so blunt when you are grieving, but you must see that Pickington's death means that you can go home now."

She stared at her hands as tears welled in her eyes. He didn't understand. How could he? He had no way of knowing that she'd been the one to push Pickington. That she was responsible for his death.

What if there was an investigation? What if it was deemed murder? What if—?

"Do you hear me, Eloise?"

A growl ripped from her throat at his condescending tone. Oh, but how she despised that tone. She hated how condescending he sounded, but mostly she hated how familiar that tone was. That autocratic, sanctimonious tone.

She clenched the duvet in her hands as she struggled for calm. But it was like a curtain had been ripped open tonight, and now she could not unsee just how much she hated her circumstances.

Her whole life had been spent being told what to do, how to do it, what to say and when to say it. Never to speak unless spoken to, and to never, ever dare to have dreams of her own.

Her parents' dreams were her dreams. And then it would be her husband's life she was living, and his commands she'd be bound to obey.

"Eloise?" he asked. No doubt he wasn't accustomed to young ladies *growling* at him.

"Don't talk to me like I'm a child," she snapped. "I am not a child."

His brows arched. "Aren't you? It seems to me you've led a sheltered life, Eloise. You're an innocent and a gently bred lady, and—"

And a murderer. He'd paused in speaking and for one ridiculous moment, she was tempted to blurt out the truth of what she'd done.

"And you belong in the safety of your family," he finished.

His voice was so kind, it should be nice. But it made her want to scream because he was handling her like some spooked mare, or some hysterical old biddy.

"Is that where I belong?" Her voice was low and grim as she kept her gaze fixed on his.

"Yes." There was that kindness again...that kindness and that pity.

The sight of his pity made her chest feel far too tight.

"You shouldn't have run away," he chided softly. "But I understand why you did."

He paused. Did he expect her to coo with delight at his generous *understanding*?

"Your parents will forgive you," he added.

"You don't know that," she said, not with anger. More like derision. "You speak so well, my lord, but you do not know the first thing about me or my parents."

"I know that Rodrick is beside himself with worry," he snapped. "And your selfish actions should you choose to keep running away like a child will only make him worry that much more."

Anger was hot and liquid in her chest.

After so many hours of fear and horror...anger was delicious.

"I'm selfish, am I? Says the man who has no obligations and is about to set off on a jolly tour of the continent rather than stay here and do his duty."

His lips curved in a harsh imitation of a smile. "You say I don't know you? I assure you, Miss Haverford, you do not know the first thing about me. Don't you dare to judge—"

"Why not?" She bolted off the bed and found herself so close their clothes were touching. She swallowed hard as a surge of nerves made her belly quiver. "Why can't I judge you when you have no problem casting judgment on me?"

"I am not the one who ran away," he said.

"And have you never done anything rash?" Her brows arched when she caught a flicker of awareness in his eyes. She'd hit upon something, all right. "Have you really never done something merely because it felt right even if it was wrong?"

He stared at her for a moment, and for a second she saw so many vying emotions in his eyes that she couldn't begin to name them. And then they were all gone, and a cynical amusement took its place. "Well, I've never broken into someone's home and stolen from them before, if that's what you mean."

Anger spiked, but more than that, she felt a surge of disappointment. In *him*, of all things. Which made no sense at all. She had no reason to expect anything from this man. Even less reason to think he might truly understand.

With a sad weight settling in her belly, she acknowledged that it was no use holding out hope that Alex might help her.

He wouldn't.

Perhaps if she explained to him about how she'd accidentally killed his uncle...

But no. That was likely a secret best kept to herself.

But as she stood there, feeling his silence settling over her like a weighted cloak, she had to face another truth. She couldn't go home to her parents. Even if she didn't fear being charged with murder, there was no going back to the life she'd fled.

It would mean the end for her. She knew that now.

It made her too low just thinking about it. Because even with Pickington gone, there would be another gentleman. A backup. A new title to win for her father, and more strings being pulled so she would dance around the society scene like the good marionette that she was.

Her sigh of defeat was genuine when she turned her face to gaze up at Alex, even if her words were a lie. "You're right," she said.

His gaze flickered left and right as if reading her expression. "I am?"

She forced a small smile. "I thank you for your assistance tonight."

"Yes, well...yes." His voice was gruff and low.

She waited for him to say something more, it seemed like he might.

He didn't.

"You're right," she said again, even as the words scraped at her throat. But a new plan was forming and the sooner she left his presence the better.

She wasn't sure she could keep up this docile act a moment longer.

A lifetime of playing the part and now she could barely maintain it for a full minute.

"With Pickington gone, I ought to go home. I shall come up with some excuse to explain my absence."

"Yes," Alex said eagerly, clearly leaping on her new plan. "Perhaps you could tell them you'd seen Pickington's death and had a nervous spell."

She stared at him.

"Right. You never swoon."

She pinched her lips together. He was enjoying her surrender far too much.

"You could tell them you were overset with excitement for your nuptials that you hid in a closet."

She blinked. "A closet."

He shrugged. "Or perhaps—"

"Perhaps it would be best if I come up with the lie," she said.

He gave a huff of amusement. "Very well. Allow me to escort you home. I'll just, er…"

He looked down at his half-dressed state and she blushed, looking away.

"I will wait for you downstairs, shall I?"

"Yes. That would be best."

She nodded, already heading to the door. Her pace quickened as she headed to a window at the front of the house.

What she saw had a grin tugging at her lips. He hadn't been lying. His trunks were already packed. And he had one of those large imperial storage trunks atop the carriage for the larger items.

Perfect.

"Ready?" Alex's voice caught her by surprise. He'd dressed quickly indeed. "I've already summoned the driver. He was already up and ready to take me on my journey. But if you need a moment..."

"I suppose I am ready now." She forced herself to adopt a sad smile, which she wore bravely during the short carriage ride to her family's home.

"Around back, if you please," she said.

Alex conveyed as much to the driver.

He went to help her out, but she stopped him. "I'll be all right from here. I know how to sneak in undetected."

He arched a brow and the look he gave her made her belly quiver all over again.

"A lady of such unique talents," he murmured.

She smiled. She certainly hoped so. She'd need all the talents she could get if she were to pull off this next step of the plan. "Thank you again for everything. And, Alex..."

She hesitated, nibbling on her lip as if this next part truly worried her.

He moved in closer. "What is it?"

"You are to meet up with Rodrick now? To search for...me?"

"Yes. At Pickington's place." He arched his brows. "Would you like me to tell him you are at home—"

"No!" She cleared her throat. "That is...no, thank you. Then you would be forced to explain how you knew where I was and..."

"Quite right," he said with a wince as she trailed off. "I'll at least try to send him home early. Tell him to check to see if you've returned while we continue, something like that."

She nodded. "That will do."

With what she hoped was her most charming smile, she

added, "And please, don't dally too long. I'd hate to think I've held up your journey after all you've done for me tonight."

He grinned. "I promise not to search for you too long."

She returned his grin. "Good night."

His smile turned softer, his eyes warming with something like affection. Maybe tenderness. Definitely a hint of regret...

"I hope it all works out for you in the end, Eloise."

She nodded. "Thank you."

She stepped out of the carriage and turned back to see him watching her with a frown. She forced her smile to be even brighter.

"Farewell, Eloise."

"Farewell," she called back softly.

But not for long.

9

*I*t was a miserable carriage ride.

He'd set out later than intended, so not a good start there. And the roads were brutal. Alex scowled out at the early morning sun, as if it was to blame for all this jostling which made sleep impossible.

He scrubbed a hand over dry, stinging eyes.

Yes, the jostling. That was all that kept him from sleeping. Certainly not guilt.

He sighed as he dropped his hand and let his head fall back against the seat. This journey was supposed to be the start of a new adventure. This was supposed to be fun.

And here he was stewing in guilt like a fool.

He wasn't sure Rodrick would ever forgive him if he were to learn the truth. Standing by and watching his poor friend driven to distraction with fears for his sister's safety.

The friends Rodrick had rallied—all their chums since their school days—they'd been tense with concern as well. They'd been worried for Rodrick's sake as well as Eloise's.

And all the while, Alex had kept silent. Whenever he

could, he suggested that Rodrick had best head home to check in, to see if she'd come home.

But the stubborn man wouldn't hear of it. His father would have sent someone if she'd returned, he kept saying.

Alex's jaw worked as he stared out the window at the passing scenery. Their blasted father. Alex didn't know the man well, but well enough. Between the stories he'd heard from Rodrick and what he now knew of Eloise's plight, it was clear the man didn't have much concern for his children's happiness.

He scowled at the memory of Rodrick's pale face and strained features.

Their father wasn't even considerate enough to allay his son's fears once Eloise returned home.

He sighed and scrubbed a hand over his face again as the image of sparkling blue eyes and lush, pink lips came to mind.

He'd been trying his best not to think of her these past few hours, but it was no use. Eloise was haunting him, and it was thoughts of her even more than Rodrick that had his gut churning with poisonous guilt.

The driver's voice sounded in the distance. They were nearly to the first posting inn where they'd change horses. One leg of the journey down. He was well on his way now.

So why was he tempted to tell the driver to turn right back around and head home?

There she was again, in his mind's eye. Smiling and sweet, her blonde hair forming a halo about her head as she said farewell with that resigned, sad little smile.

His heart twisted mercilessly.

What sort of monster lets a woman face her fate alone like that?

But then again, what else could he do?

And suddenly his mind scrambled to come up with

options. *You could have given her the coin she'd been after and sent her on her way.* It might not have been safe, but it was what she'd wanted.

You could have taken her with you.

You could have told Rodrick the truth from the start and convinced him to help her.

You could have...

He shut that voice down with a ruthless smack.

She's not your problem. Her happiness is not your concern.

That was what he told himself. Over and over he said it. But his nagging conscience wouldn't cease. He kept seeing the sadness in her eyes, and the anger too.

Would her parents forgive her? At least his vile old uncle was out of the equation—cruel as that thought might be. But would they find some new gentleman for her to marry?

Would he be even worse?

Alex shifted uneasily, his gaze catching on the inn up ahead but his mind back in London with Eloise.

Lud, what if her parents decided they still wanted her to be a countess? There were few people Alex detested more than his deceased uncle, but the other uncle, the heir—he was a close second.

Thoughts of the younger uncle who would now inherit the title of Earl of Pickington had Alex sneering. Oh yes, his relations up north would be celebrating right about now.

It was no secret that the brothers had been feuding for years and the younger brother had always coveted the title. Alex's father had been the youngest, and potentially the worst of the three. But when he'd died years ago, Alex had ceased taking any interest in family squabbles.

He still didn't care what became of that title or his cruel family. But if Eloise was involved...

No, he still didn't care.

His churning gut begged to differ.

He couldn't stop imagining his loathsome uncle with Eloise. He wouldn't treat her the way she deserved, that much was certain.

But perhaps they'd all learn from her escapades. Perhaps her parents would take her wishes into consideration and they'd find her a nice, handsome young gentleman who would be kind to her and—

A growl escaped his lips before he could stop it, and then he was forced to stare down at his clenched fists in horror.

Why did that image make him want to rip apart the carriage interior with his bare hands?

It made no sense. But he couldn't have denied this surge of hot angry possessiveness if he tried.

He hated the thought of Eloise marrying another man. Any other man.

And that was...

Insanity.

He'd lost his mind.

Clearly, he needed sleep and he needed it badly. His brain had grown utterly addled.

The carriage rumbled to a stop and Alex was quick to leap out. Perhaps some ale was what he needed. Yes, it was still early hours yet, but he needed something to drown out this guilt. Something to drive away all thoughts of Eloise and her future and her brother and...

Oh blast.

He needed some sort of escape from this torture.

The inn was full despite the early hour. It stank of body odor and horse sweat, and dust seemed to cover every surface of the dimly lit tavern. But they served ale, and that was what mattered at the moment.

By the time the horses were changed, Alex was no less miserable, still riddled with guilt, but so exhausted between the ale and a sleepless night that he stumbled back to the carriage gratefully, ready to fling himself down onto the seat and into the blessed oblivion of sleep.

Or rather, that was what he would have done, if he hadn't thrown open the carriage door to find it already occupied.

He stood there for a long moment, certain that he'd lost his mind altogether.

The ale was poisoned.

Or he had died and this was heaven.

Those were the only explanations he could conjure for how he'd come to find Eloise sitting in his carriage, her hands folded neatly in her lap as she greeted him with a smile.

"Eloise?" His voice was raspy and soft, like he wasn't quite certain he wanted to acknowledge this vision.

He could very well end up in a madhouse.

"My lord." She nodded politely, but there was no denying the mischievous amusement in her eyes.

At his expense. She was also rumpled, her hair a mess and her gown thoroughly ruined. But still stunningly beautiful all the same.

"How..." He started. "Where... What..."

Her smile grew. "Miss me?"

His mouth opened and closed a few times, and she appeared to lose patience. "Do come in and shut the carriage door, Alex. I'd rather not cause a scene, if you don't mind."

He blinked.

So polite. So genteel.

"Are you real?" he asked.

She laughed. "Just come inside and shut the door so we can be on our way."

On our way.

Those were the incongruous words that finally managed to jar him out of his addled state.

"You stowed away?" he said in disbelief.

But he did, in fact, follow her orders. He climbed inside just as the driver hoisted himself up to his seat.

As if by some unspoken agreement, they waited for the carriage to start moving before either of them spoke again.

"You stowed away in my carriage," he said, his voice firmer and louder now that he was certain he wasn't hallucinating.

"I did," she said.

"How?"

She pointed to the roof of the carriage. "Your trunk is large and I am small."

He blinked. "You..." His brows arched as a new thought struck. "What of my belongings?"

She had the good grace to flinch. "You may need to borrow a few items when you first arrive."

"You...you..." He stopped speaking because he wasn't at all certain if he wanted to shout or laugh.

Both seemed equally likely to erupt out of him at any moment. So instead, he fell silent.

"You have far more nerve than I'd suspected," he finally said.

She pursed her lips as she nodded. "It would appear that I do." After a moment, her gaze grew distant and she added, "Though I'm not quite certain if it's bravery or desperation."

"I'm not sure a distinction is necessary," he said.

She smiled. So sweet. So good. But...but not weak. Not helpless. And most certainly not the fragile, spineless creature he'd thought her to be.

No simpering, docile fool would take it upon herself to hide away in a trunk to avoid an unwanted marriage.

Certainly, his mother never would have had such nerve.

And there... There it was. His mind finally veered to the one place he'd been trying his best not to revisit. The memories that Eloise had stirred in him from the first moment he'd seen her.

His mother.

He'd been battling thoughts of her all morning. Eloise had reminded him of her when they'd first met. So much that it was impossible to look upon her with any objectivity. For thoughts of memories brought with them emotions too complicated to name.

But now...

He stared at her unblinking for several long moments.

Well, now Eloise didn't remind him of his mother. Not at all. In fact, all he could see was just how different she and his mother were in character...even if they'd found themselves in similar circumstances.

I'm not sure if it's bravery or desperation, she'd said.

"Perhaps desperation is what forces us to see what we're made of," he said at last, though he was mostly talking to himself. His voice was far too gruff and low. It sounded oddly intimate in these close quarters.

Alarm rang through him and he muttered an oath that made Eloise blush. "You do know how this will look for me if we are caught, do you not?"

She winced. "Yes. And I am sorry about that."

"Oh, you're sorry, are you?" Anger laced his voice.

She shrugged. "I am sorry. But also..." She pressed her lips together for a moment. "I've realized that there is no one in this world who is going to take my wishes into consideration. Which means, I must look after myself."

And just like that, his anger was replaced with a swift, nauseating bout of guilt.

"Your brother—"

"Loves me, yes I know," she said. "And it pains me greatly that I'll be worrying him. But in the end, it is not his fate at stake, is it?"

He opened his mouth but had no idea how to respond. No, she was right on that count. However... "It is *my* future at stake, though, Miss Haverford. If we were to be caught together... Your brother will call me out, you know. Friend or not, he'll—"

"He won't," she interrupted tersely. "Not if I explain."

"Then we would be married, at the very least." He arched both brows. "You do understand that, do you not?"

Her reaction to that proposition was instant and...startling.

He'd admit, he'd expected a different reaction. Perhaps shame, fear, maybe even a little guilt.

What he got was rage.

Her cheeks turned crimson and her eyes flashed with lightning as she leaned forward and spoke through gritted teeth. "I truly despise that tone of yours," she snarled.

He leaned back in surprise. "What tone?"

"The tone that says you think me to be a child."

Defensive anger had him shooting back, "Only a child runs away from home, love."

She narrowed her eyes. "There you are wrong, my lord. Only children and grown women who are treated like children run from their homes. Because that is the only option left to us."

He scoffed, but before he could protest, she continued, "What other choice do I have? Honestly. Do you think pleading with my parents will change their mind? If you think that, you'd best have a chat with my sister Charlotte. No amount of fighting got her out of her arranged marriage—"

"But—"

"Yes, yes, she was fortunate enough to fall in love with her husband. But I do not have the same high hopes. So then, what do you propose I do?"

"Well, whatever it is, I just ask that it has nothing to do with me."

He felt churlish and mean as soon as the words escaped. A gallant, chivalrous knight he was most definitely not.

But then again, he'd already known that, hadn't he? His mother had been wretched with misery in her marriage, and what had he done to help her?

Nothing. He'd left.

But then again, what had she ever done to help him?

He looked away, unable to meet Eloise's disdainful glare. But he couldn't drown out her voice.

"Do not fret, my lord." Her voice was still light and sweet as ever, but it oozed with disdain. "I have no interest in marrying you either. We will not be caught, and if we are, I will find a means to escape. Heaven forbid *you* are forced into a marriage. I cannot imagine how dreadful that would be for you."

He shot her a narrowed-eyed glare. "Acerbic wit does not suit you, Miss Haverford."

She smirked in response. "Perhaps not. It's new to me, you know." She tilted her head to the side, her animosity fading. "It's odd, really..."

"What is?"

"Taking the reins of one's own life after nearly twenty years of being a puppet."

"A puppet."

Her smile was small and sad. "I've always seen myself as a marionette. You know, the dolls with strings that they have at the fair?"

He gave a grunt of acknowledgement.

"Well, today I have decided to cut the strings."

He felt a surge of...something he did not like. It was soft and sweet and made his chest feel too tight and warm. It was affection of a sort. Maybe even a little pride.

Not that he'd done anything to help her. What did he have to be proud of?

"If that's the case, then you ought to be able to face your family."

She nibbled on her lip. "Maybe," she murmured at last.

He suspected there was much more she was not telling him, but he didn't wish to hear it anyway.

And yet he shifted in his seat waiting for her to speak with more than a hint of impatience. "What is it?" he finally snapped.

She gave a weary sigh. "It's best if you do not know everything, my lord. I will keep my secrets and you shall maintain your independence, and just as soon as we're aboard a ship to the continent, I will be well out of your hair."

He stared at her in dismay. "You mean to travel the continent unchaperoned? Without a guide?"

"I will find my family soon enough."

"How?" he snapped. And now it was fear, plain and simple, that had his chest tightening. Truly, this girl was maddening. She might be stronger and far more clever than he'd suspected, but she was still aggravatingly naive. "You will come to harm—"

"I am not your concern, remember?" They sat there glaring for a long moment, before she softened with another sigh. "You look awful, Alex. Get some sleep."

He could say the same for her. She had dark circles beneath her eyes and her hair was mussed, her clothes rumpled and torn...

But then again, he couldn't say she looked awful. Because that would be a lie.

She looked more beautiful than he'd ever seen her.

She had pride and confidence and bravery and...

Oh curse it.

He turned away from her with a huff. He could admire

the chit while still knowing her to be in the wrong, couldn't he?

He watched from the corner of his eyes as she lost the battle with sleep first. Despite his exhaustion, he couldn't follow her into slumber. When they reached the next stop, Eloise slept through it all.

She missed the fact that they'd stopped at all. She missed it when he got out of the coach. And she didn't hear him call for the innkeeper.

"I have a message that needs to be sent," he said, keeping one eye on the carriage where Eloise slept. "I'll pay whatever it takes, but I need a message sent to the Viscount Henley posthaste."

Rodrick would come for her. And he'd know what to do. He'd help plead her case and find her someone more suitable and...

He turned away from the carriage with a rough sigh.

Oh curse it. He wouldn't waste another moment second guessing his decision. Because Eloise had been right. No one else was going to look out for her future but her, and it was his responsibility to look after himself.

He'd always known that but today she'd made it clear.

It was every man for himself.

10

*E*loise stood by meekly as Alex dealt with the innkeeper.

"...and I'll need an adjoining room for my sister," he was saying.

She peeked up at him. The man was adept at lying, she'd give him that.

Guilt rippled through her. She truly did not enjoy putting him in this position.

And now that position was made even worse because they'd arrived at the docks only to find that the weather was not suitable for crossing, and they'd have to wait until it cleared.

So now they were here. For who knew how long. And Alex was forced to claim her as his sister and hope that no one caught them together lest his life be ruined.

Oh yes, guilt was definitely weighing on her now.

She straightened her shoulders as she reminded herself of what she'd told him only that morning, early on in the journey.

No one else was looking out for her future or her happiness, so it was up to her. The fact that Alex had been dragged into this was unfortunate but...well, needs must, and all that.

This reasoning did little to assuage her guilt. Or her fears. Or her worry for Rodrick and her parents, or...

She shook her head, forcing those thoughts aside. She'd made her decision the moment she'd fled from Pickington's home. And she'd made it all over again when she'd snuck onto Alex's carriage rather than return home.

Her decision had been made, the course set. The only way forward was to continue on this path.

"You must be cold and hungry after your journey," the innkeeper's wife said to Alex, sparing a curious glance in Eloise's direction before adding. "I'll prepare the rooms and bring you some food if you and your...sister wish to wait by the fire."

Eloise flinched. Was it her imagination or was there a hint of mocking in the woman's tone when she'd called her his sister?

She clenched her hands at her sides, her cheeks burning. She'd best get used to it, she supposed. She was scandalous now. Traveling alone on the continent, running away from her family...

She was ruined. And whether or not her motives were good hardly mattered. From this moment on, she could expect to be judged and found wanting. Even by a lowly innkeeper's wife.

The innkeeper's daughter was watching them as well, but she from a short distance away and with a rather dazed look on her face that Eloise could well understand. Indeed, the young girl's lips were parted with awe as she watched Alex hand some coins to her father.

Alex was dashing to begin with. But something about the stubble that darkened his strong jawline and the rumpled state of his clothes...

He still looked every bit the gentleman, of course, but with a breathtaking hint of the rogue about him as well. He turned to Eloise with an equally roguish smile. "Well, sister, shall we warm ourselves by the fire?"

The innkeeper's wife led them to a small antechamber in the back of the inn that was alarmingly empty aside from a few tables and chairs, and a roaring fire.

"I'll bring your meal shortly," the innkeeper's wife said with a smile as she backed out of the small, blissfully warm room.

They were alone.

Eloise's heart fluttered dangerously as she glanced over at Alex. This was hardly the first time they'd been alone together. They'd been alone in one another's company all day and for the better part of last night.

But this felt...different.

Perhaps because they were at an inn. Or because for the first time in her life she was far from her family's protection.

For the first time ever she was truly on her own.

Alone...but for Alex. Her knees began to tremble. Hunger, she decided, as she sank into the settee that had been situated before the fire.

But she knew that wasn't true.

She was hungry, yes, but this shaky feeling, the overwhelming emotions that were attempting to rear up from the dark corners where she'd pushed them...

That was what had her shaking.

Alex came to stand beside her, holding his hands out toward the flame.

The silence seemed to stretch and tighten between them until Eloise's heart was pounding frantically as she waited for him to break it.

Why was she suddenly so nervous around him? It made no sense. But no, it wasn't just nerves. It was something else.

Something far more dangerous. Whatever it was, it made her keenly aware of his scent, masculine and warm, and now so familiar to her she knew without a doubt she'd miss it when he was gone.

She'd be homesick for it.

Which was ridiculous, of course.

But this tension between them grew as he shifted, moving toward her and then settling onto the settee beside her.

She could have sworn she felt the heat from him more acutely than the fire that roared in front of them.

Again, ridiculous.

She was exhausted, that was all. Tired and hungry and...

And scared. Oh, she was so very terrified right now. But there were so many reasons she couldn't even pinpoint why. Because she was on her own. Because of the unknown adventure that lay ahead. Because she was alone with Alex. Because he would be leaving her just as soon as he could...

"Are you all right?" His voice was low and gruff, and his gaze was fixed on her hands, which were twisted in her skirts, her knuckles white.

She nodded.

He sighed heavily. "It has been a long day, but the rooms should be ready soon."

She nodded again.

"You must be hungry."

Another nod. She didn't entirely trust herself to speak.

"Eloise..." The wariness in his voice had her lifting her gaze to his. She immediately wished she hadn't. His gaze was filled with concern. Reluctant, perhaps, but it was concern all the same.

And all at once, she lost the battle. Tears welled up before she could stop them, and a hiccupy little sob escaped. She dipped her head as if she could hide the fact that she was crying.

"Eloise," he said again as he sank to the floor before her, on his knees as he reached for her hands. From this position he could see her face clearly despite her attempt to hide. "Please don't cry."

She tried to tell him she was sorry but only a pathetic little whimper escaped.

"Please," he said again, desperation in his eyes as he moved to sit beside her. "Don't cry, El. I don't know what to do for you when you cry."

El. She sniffled. The sound of a nickname from his lips felt absurdly...normal. Natural, even. She supposed running away with a man had a way of creating intimacy where there was once none.

"You don't have to do anything," she managed in a watery voice. "I am not your responsibility."

He gave a huff of wry amusement. "Aren't you?"

The words stung. Because of course she was. With no money, no clothes, no horse or carriage of her own...she was at his mercy. It was only his reluctant kindness and no doubt his affection for her brother that had gotten her this far.

"I am sorry, you know," she said.

A hint of a smile tugged at his lips. "For crying? Don't be. You've been through quite an ordeal. I'd say you're allowed a few tears. It's my own fault that I can't abide weeping."

"Your fault?" she echoed as she swiped at her cheeks.

His lips were still curved up, but she caught a flicker of dark emotions. "It reminds me of my childhood, I suppose. Not in a good way."

Questions rose up, but his gaze grew guarded. She could practically see him pulling away from her at the mention of his childhood.

So she settled for, "I should think not." When he arched a brow in question, she added, "Weeping would suggest that these are not happy memories."

"Indeed, they are not," he said with a forced cheerfulness as he changed the tone. "So, tell me how I can make this weeping stop."

A huff of laughter broke through her tears.

"A new gown?" he offered. "Some sweets or...or a poem, perhaps? I've heard ladies like poems."

He was teasing and she knew it. Just like she knew he was playing the fool just to distract her from her troubles.

"If only it were that easy," she said with a laugh. "Alas, I'm afraid what troubles me cannot be fixed with a poem."

"Mmm, I had a feeling perhaps that was the case." He grew serious as he squeezed her hands. "But if there is anything I can do..."

She sniffed back more tears at his kindness. "You've already done more than enough. Thank you for my shelter tonight, and..." She drew in a deep breath. "And for paying for my passage tomorrow?"

His brows arched, his eyes glinting with laughter. "Was that your way of asking me to pay your way?"

She pressed her lips together. The biggest flaw in this plan was that she still had no coin to her name. All she had was this evening gown which was tattered and wrinkled from the journey...and utterly impractical for all the travel to come.

She hated relying on him so, but until she got to Charlotte, she had no other means.

A fact he well knew because his gaze grew cunning. "I never promised to pay your way, El."

"Yes, but...but surely you would not just leave me here..." She trailed off in question.

She caught a flicker of emotions she didn't like in his eyes. Guilt, pity, and maybe even regret.

Because he'd helped her this far? Was he worried about

what her brother would say? Or perhaps how much he was risking for her?

"Eloise, I'm not..." He thrust a hand through his hair with a muttered curse and his gaze drifted away from hers toward the fire. "I'm not going to leave you here."

Her heart leapt with hope and...something else.

There it was again, this odd yearning sensation. Like she was homesick, but not for her parents and not for her home...but for him.

Which made no sense at all. And yet she couldn't deny it.

He made her feel this yearning sensation. He made her want something that she couldn't describe. That she didn't even know how to put into words.

When he turned back to face her, the firelight reflected in his eyes, and she could not read his thoughts or emotions. "Will you not miss your parents if you leave? What about your brother?"

She toyed with the material of her gown. How to tell him that she was nearly certain she'd murdered his uncle, so they'd likely not want her back. She would only bring trouble if she were to stay.

"I love my parents," she said slowly. "And Rodrick, of course, but..."

He arched his brows when she came to a stop. He waited patiently and she took a moment to gather the thoughts that had been swirling all night.

"When I was a little girl, I told my mother I wanted to be a knight."

His brows hitched up further, a smile hovering over his lips expectantly. "A knight?"

She grinned at the memory. "Yes. Our governess had been reading us these fairytale stories before bedtime, and I wanted to be the knight." She shrugged, her cheeks flushing with heat under his watchful stare. "But when I told my mother, she laughed and explained that I was the princess in the story. Not the brave stoic knight who saved the day, but the helpless damsel in distress whose sole purpose in the tale was to be pretty and kind and...and pretty." She wrinkled her nose. "That's all that was required of her."

He tilted his head to the side as if seeing her in a new light but said nothing.

"My entire life all I ever wanted was to make my parents happy," she said. "No, to make them *proud*." The word sounded bitter on her tongue. "The only time that happened was when they talked about my...my..." She dipped her head with embarrassment.

But Alex seemed to understand because his voice held a hint of laughter as he supplied, "Your beauty?"

She nodded, her cheeks burning. "All they wanted from me was a good match, and they were so pleased with Lord Pickington and..." She wet her lips and cast a look at Alex.

A memory reared of him calling her a child and she flinched. "I suppose you think me unbearably spoiled. I was raised well and given everything a girl could ask for, and yet I couldn't go through with the one task that was asked of me."

"I don't think you're spoiled," he said slowly, his gaze thoughtful. "I think you grew up. I think you realized that there was more to life than your parents' hopes and dreams."

She nodded, her heart clenching painfully with gratitude that he did not judge. "That is it exactly. Do you know... Oh, of course you know, he was your uncle..." She sighed in exasperation with herself. "He'd had two wives already. Two. And I know nothing of them. No one speaks of them, and I don't recall ever seeing them. I do not know their names, only that they were formerly known as Lady Pickington."

He grimaced as though he could see where this was going and felt for her.

"All at once last night, I realized that I would be the same. Forgotten. No longer my own person. Just another in a line of nameless, faceless, spiritless ladies who were given to that man to sire an heir, and I couldn't bear it." She bit her lip as she looked to Alex anxiously, hoping he would understand. "It felt like a fate worse than death. I'd be losing myself just as surely as if I'd died. Does that...does that make sense?"

He nodded, his eyes grim and the set of his jaw hard.

For a moment she thought he wouldn't speak, and when he did, she was startled by the ferocity in his tone. "It would have been hell on earth. I know because I saw my mother suffer the same fate."

She blinked in surprise, her lips parting at the pain she saw in his gaze. "Oh, Alex," she murmured.

He turned away and took a deep breath. "My father was cruel. To both of us, my mother and me. But in different ways. I think..." He cleared his throat, his jaw working. "I used to blame her..." His frown made his dark brows furrow. "No, that's not right. I didn't blame her, necessarily, but I..." His throat worked as he swallowed. "I never understood why she didn't try to protect herself...or me."

Or me. Eloise's heart twisted mercilessly at that last bit, tacked on as if it was an afterthought, and not a heartbreaking question for his mother.

"What happened to her?"

"She took her own life," he said. "I'd left."

She wasn't even sure he knew how much guilt she could see in his eyes and etched into every line of his face as he cleared his throat and continued. "I'd left my father's house just as soon as I was able. I left her there alone, and she...she did not survive."

Her breath caught as her heart lurched. "Oh, Alex, I'm so sorry."

"So was I," he said, his tone bitter and rueful. "I was sorry for her and for myself. But then, after a time, I found it was easier to be angry. At my father, who died not long after, at myself for not saving her, and..." His nostrils flared and his eyes grew dark with emotions as he met her gaze. "And at her for not being brave. For not leaving to save herself, even if it meant leaving me behind."

Eloise could hear her own heartbeat in the silence that followed, and for a moment she felt certain she could feel the confusing swirl of emotions she saw in his eyes.

"So yes," he said, his voice gruff. "I understand why you ran. And I commend you for having the strength to do so."

She frowned because his voice grew stilted and his gaze wouldn't quite meet hers.

"But that doesn't mean I think you're making the right decision in fleeing from your family."

"Don't you?" Confusion had her squinting at him in the firelight. "After all you've just said, after what I've told you...I think you know that I cannot go back."

His jaw worked. "Fine. Perhaps I do. But..."

She understood before he even found the words. "But you don't wish to be involved," she said. "Yes, I understand that. And I don't wish to drag you into my mess any further than I already have."

His gaze was heavy on her now, but she couldn't meet his gaze. This hurt sensation...it was silly. She had no reason to be hurt or to feel rejected. It wasn't like they were friends. They barely knew one another. He owed her nothing.

"Eloise, you should know..." He paused, and then was interrupted completely when the innkeeper's wife barged in with a tray filled with food.

"Here you are," she said, her brisk tone breaking the heated, intimate moment as surely as a cold gust of wind. "Enjoy your food. Your rooms will be waiting for you when you're ready."

11

He had to tell her.

Alex eyed Eloise over the table as she dug into the stew with relish. He'd be doing the same if guilt wasn't currently eating him alive from the inside out.

He'd made the right decision in sending a messenger for Rodrick.

Hadn't he?

So then, why had guilt been weighing upon him like a boulder all day?

It was because of his mother, no doubt. His memories of her and the emotions they stirred had him acting without thought when it came to Eloise. There was no denying the similarities. He'd seen it that first moment they'd met. As they'd danced, he'd been repelled by it. She'd seemed so like his mother in all the worst ways. So helpless. So docile. So weak.

But he'd been so very wrong in that first assessment. She was nothing like his mother. He knew without having to reason it through that if Eloise had been in his mother's position, she would have moved hell and earth to protect her son. To protect herself as well.

That was what she'd been doing when she ran, and here he was, just waiting to offer her back to her family like a pet that'd gotten loose.

She smiled at him. "Aren't you hungry? You've barely eaten a thing."

"I am, yes, I was just..." He cleared his throat and looked away. "Just thinking."

He felt her gaze on him as he ate.

"I am truly sorry, Alex," she said softly.

He glanced up in surprise.

"You did not deserve what I did to you." She leaned forward, determination in her gaze making them sparkle and glow like gems. "And I promise, I won't let you pay for my reckless actions."

He arched a brow. "Really? Because it sounds as though I'll be paying for everything."

She blushed at his teasing. "I meant—"

"I know what you meant," he said. And for some reason it made his gut feel too heavy. She wanted to protect him. From having to marry her.

Nothing about that felt right, and not because he had some latent chivalrous side to him that he'd never noticed before.

He didn't realize he'd been staring at her so intently until she began to fidget.

"Hopefully it will never be a concern. No one knows I am with you, and so long as we board that ship tomorrow, we will be on our way with no one the wiser. Right?"

Wrong. Her brother would be here. Even now he was likely riding roughshod to save his sister from her own reckless actions.

Alex's stomach twisted angrily.

What was even more strange, aside from the guilt and the second guessing of his decision, every time he thought of sending her away, he felt an ache deep in his chest. Almost like he'd miss her.

Which was ridiculous, of course. He barely knew her. She'd been nothing but trouble. And amusing, he'd give her that. He hadn't quite realized how bored he'd become with his lonely lifestyle until she'd burst into it, surprising him at every turn and making him swing between laughter, anger, and an aggravating desire with every passing second.

The desire he didn't dare to acknowledge. Not even to himself. It would be far too easy to forget himself here at this inn, where no one knew them. Where they had perfect solitude and this strange, and ever-growing intimacy between them.

But even as he told himself to ignore it, he found his gaze dipping to her full lips.

Just one taste...

What would be the harm in one little kiss?

He shut down those thoughts and focused on his meal.

"Once we are on the continent, I assure you I will leave you alone," she continued.

She seemed to have misconstrued his silence and his gaze darted up in alarm. "You mean to travel alone?"

"With a chaperone," she said quickly. "And not for long. I ought to be able to track down my sister and aunt quickly enough. I'll head to my aunt's estate first and then...then..."

For a moment her gaze grew distant and she looked lost. Overwhelmed by all that was to come. She recovered quickly and her smile was bright. "Well, then I shall seek them out and I have no doubt they will welcome me."

He studied her for a long moment. He hated this plan. *Despised* it. And not just because it was dangerous.

He hated knowing that she'd be ruined, not welcome

back in London society. He hated knowing that her relationship with Rodrick would be strained at best, and that she'd be cutting ties to her life here entirely.

She deserved better than to be cast off as some scandalous runaway bride.

But mostly...

Mostly he hated that he'd never see her again.

His brows furrowed with the unpleasant realization. When had he become so attached to this woman who he'd held in such disdain only the evening before?

But that had been before.

Before she'd shocked him and earned his respect. Before she'd made him laugh. Before he'd found himself opening up about his childhood, which he never told anyone about.

But he trusted her not to wield it against him, just like he knew she would understand. He fell back in his seat as the pieces fell into place with a jarring jolt.

He liked her. He really, truly liked her. Maybe...more than liked her.

She bit her lip, her spoon hovering over her dish. "Why are you staring at me like that?"

"I'm just...just thinking," he said. "About your plan."

She winced. "I'll admit, it's not a terribly well thought out plan. But..." She shrugged with a rueful smile. "I haven't had a whole lot of time to think this through."

Exactly, he ought to say. *This is too impulsive and impetuous. And this is precisely why you should go straight back home to your family.*

But he didn't say that. Instead, he leaned forward, curiosity getting the best of him. "What is it that you want, Eloise?"

She blinked, her lips working before she sputtered, "Pardon?"

He pushed the food aside and folded his arms over the

narrow table. "What is it that you want? If there were no impediments, and no demands from your family, and…" He shook his head, curiosity burning him alive now because…because…

Curse it. He wanted her to have the life she wanted.

No, he wanted to help her have it.

Oh for the love of…

He wanted to be the one to give it to her.

His hard stare was one of shock now as his insides reverberated with this new realization. What had she done to him? He sat here, his chair on solid ground, but he had the unnerving sensation that the world had flipped upside down.

"What do I want?" Her eyes were wide as she dropped her spoon with a clatter.

One might have thought he'd asked her if she wanted to dance naked under the moon. She couldn't have sounded more surprised.

"That was the question, yes."

Rueful laughter warmed her eyes and made her lips curve up so very sweetly.

His heart gave an alarming thud as he watched her think over her response. She was very sincere. So genuine. So…guileless, that was the word to describe her. He'd been wrong to think her docile or meek. But she was sheltered, and she was innocent, and despite her good manners and her calm, kind demeanor, there was no hint of artifice about her.

Certainly not when she was alone with him.

He could see her mind whirring as she turned over his words.

"Is it really such a difficult question?" he asked.

"No," she said quickly. "I mean, yes. I mean…" She gave a huff of exasperation that made him laugh. "I mean, I have never considered it. Not since I was a child." Her gaze met his and he felt the connection like a punch to the gut.

She shrugged. "No one has ever asked me that before."

His heart twisted. What a pity. This marvel of a girl had never once been asked what she wanted...what would make her happy. He leaned forward even farther, tickled when she pushed her bowl to the side to do the same. The table was so narrow that their elbows touched and her lips were tantalizingly close to his.

"I suppose..." She wet her lips, and he fought back a groan in response.

She wasn't trying to tempt him, this much was obvious. Yet she was still temptation itself sitting here all disheveled, yet glowing more brightly than the sun.

"I want to marry," she said slowly. "And I want a family." She smiled soft and sweet, her eyes filled with such affection that his heart swelled until his ribcage felt like a prison. "I've always wanted children."

"How many?" His voice was low and gruff, and he felt for all the world like he was caught in a dream. Her voice wrapped around him like silk, and her scent and her warmth were all that existed in the world.

"At least four," she said. Her eyes took on a faraway look, and he felt like he was seeing it too, this fantastical future she imagined. "I want a happy family, with a husband who I respect. I want a household filled with laughter and music."

He could see it so clearly, he found himself saying, "I never thought such a thing was possible before..."

Before you.

He swallowed the words. This new sentimental bent was just exhaustion taking its toll, that was all. It was the endless time alone they'd been spending in one another's company. That was the only explanation for the way he couldn't seem to get close enough, the way he found himself hanging on her every word.

"I never thought it possible either," she said softly, her

gaze meeting his.

Until you.

She didn't say it. The words were only in his head. Surely, he was imagining that he heard it there in her voice and saw it in her eyes...

She looked away and he blinked himself back to sanity.

"I want the sort of happy marriage Charlotte has found, and which Rodrick will have...if he ever summons up the courage to tell his fiancée how he feels."

She added the last part under her breath, and Alex grinned. So, she'd noticed it too, then. How Rodrick was head over heels for his own fiancée. *Poor chap.*

His smile fell just as quickly because... Was that what this was?

He drew back and all at once he could see himself from an outsider's perspective. He was practically fawning over the lady, leaning over like he was and grinning like a dolt.

She was smiling at him too, as if they were in on this joke together. And he liked that.

He loved it.

This new intimacy they shared, which, if he were being honest, he'd felt growing between them ever since he'd discovered her in his study. It wasn't just being alone together, and it was more than physical attraction. It was an understanding that he'd never felt with another...and had never expected to find.

It was unnerving and...wonderful.

Like he'd found *his* person, the one that spoke his language and understood his humor. The one that saw past his masks just as he saw past hers.

He'd spent his entire childhood envying other boys who'd found this sort of connection, whether with a sibling or a cousin or a friend.

Alex had never found it, and as he'd grown older, he'd

given up hope that he ever would.

Until now.

Until Eloise.

It was remarkable to have found it here, now, with her. It was wondrous.

Not to mention, it was horrendously bad timing.

His heart lurched as he remembered what he'd meant to tell her at the start of their meal. *Rodrick is on his way. I've sent for him.*

He opened his mouth, but Eloise spoke first.

"And you?" Eloise asked. "What is it that you want?"

You. I want you. He swallowed hard. This made no sense. It was happening too quickly and there were far too many complications.

"I suppose..." He took a deep breath as he considered her and weighed his words. "I'd always thought that I wouldn't marry."

Her eyes widened. "Ever?"

He lifted a shoulder. "Perhaps eventually, when I was ready to settle down and sire an heir."

Her smile dimmed. "I see."

She didn't. That much was clear. Because if she could see what he was imagining right now, she'd likely run away in terror.

He was picturing her. And him. And children—at least four of them. He was imagining what a marriage and family might be like with a woman who was brave enough to fight for herself and her children. Who wouldn't allow him to be like his father, if those negative traits were indeed passed down as he feared.

What would it be like to be a part of that future she'd envisioned...the one that was filled with laughter and love, friendship and trust?

Trust. The word seemed to mock him. She'd trusted him

and he'd gone behind her back.

He'd told himself it was for the best when he'd sent that missive to Rodrick. That was in her best interests. But now...

Well, now he had to face the fact that it had been what was best for him. Not her. Because he'd feared being trapped into a marriage like his parents' more than anything. More than he'd cared about her happiness.

But now...

Well, now it was clear to him that he cared about her happiness so much that it seemed to drown out everything else. Because he could not be happy if she was not.

Odd, that. To have one's happiness suddenly dependent on another's.

It was so awe inspiring it left him at a loss for words.

It wasn't a bad thing, but rather...quite good.

"What is that look?" she asked, wariness in her tone.

How had he been looking? He suspected slightly crazed. He felt more than a little crazed, but also...solid. Like he'd found his footing. For the first time in his life he understood what it meant to have purpose. To have responsibilities and duties—not ones inherited with his title—but ones that came from the heart.

"I think perhaps you and I have more in common than I'd thought," he said at last.

She grinned. "Do we?"

He saw a delicate shiver race over her and she crossed her arms.

"Come, let's return to the fire," he said.

Once more they sat side by side on the settee near the fire. He wrapped an arm around her shoulders to help warm her. "That's better, isn't it?"

She nodded. "Yes. Thank you."

She sounded breathless.

He felt like there wasn't enough air to be had.

The room was small and the sound of the fire made this setting unbearably intimate. The feel of her in his arms was more intoxicating than any spirit.

She lifted her face to meet his gaze. "How are we so very alike then?"

"Just in that we've both run from our obligations and our duties. Not because we are opposed to marriage or families in and of themselves...but because they were not what we chose for ourselves."

He could feel himself hedging, the rational part of his mind reeling at what he was about to say.

"We could go back, El," he said softly.

Her lips parted as her gaze narrowed on him. "I don't know what you mean."

He cleared his throat. "Together," he clarified. "We could go back together."

He waited for understanding to dawn. If they arrived back home together, they'd be forced to wed.

They would be married.

The words 'will you marry me' were on the tip of his tongue, his heart tripping and hitching in shock at his own impulsiveness. Reason was trying to fight him on this, to tell him this was a massive decision, that he ought to think this through...

But it felt right.

And time was not on their side. And...

Oh blast. He wanted her. Here. Now. Forever. That was all there was to it.

But he would not force her into this. He'd not push her into a marriage like her parents had done. So, he resisted the urge to speak, waiting instead for her to react.

So far all she'd done was stare at him in blank silence.

And then her eyes were welling with tears once more. "I cannot, Alex. I thank you, truly...but I cannot marry you."

12

Her heart was breaking in two.

Which was ludicrous. She barely knew the man!

But that did nothing to change the fact that her heart ached at what she'd had to say. Because her very first instinct had been to say 'yes!'

He was all but offering marriage, and even if he seemed wary, even if he hadn't just told her outright that it wasn't what he wanted, she was nearly selfish enough to claim it, because...because she could *see* it.

She'd seen it so clearly in her mind's eye, she felt as if she could touch it. A future with Alex. He'd make her laugh, and she'd make him smile, and they'd discuss everything and anything with this odd intimacy that was so natural between them.

Her parents would forgive her, and Rodrick would be pleased, and her whole debacle of running from her own wedding would be forgotten.

And that was when reality had slapped her in the face.

She'd been responsible for his uncle's death. If anyone

were to discover her part in it she would be ruined, and she'd take him down with her. She'd known then that she'd have to say no...and yet she'd still paused, hoping to find a good excuse to reason away that decision.

Instead, she'd just remembered what he'd said. He hadn't wanted to marry...not now, at least. And likely not her.

He was being kind, that was all.

And she couldn't trap him into a marriage. Especially not after the way she'd murdered his uncle and all.

And so, she sat here with an aching chest and a pain in her heart as he nodded.

"Very well," he said.

He removed his arm from around her shoulders and she shivered at the cold.

Very well. That was it. No questions, no comments. But she hated the way his expression went cold, and to her horror she found herself babbling.

"I can't marry you, even if you were kind enough to consider it."

"Yes, you made that clear." His gaze wasn't quite meeting hers. "I understand."

She frowned. "But you don't."

"I think I do. You do not wish to marry me, and I cannot say I don't understand that. You were ready to flee the country to avoid marrying one of my relatives, why should you rush into a hasty marriage with the likes of me?"

Oh dear, the bitterness in his voice made her flinch. "You are nothing at all like your uncle."

"Thank you," he said, his eyes chilly now as he turned to face her, his tone too mild. "I appreciate the fact that you see the difference between my vile old uncle and myself."

She winced. "You're angry."

"No, not angry, just..." He turned away with a sigh. "It was a bad idea. Clearly."

"It wasn't." Now it was she who sounded terse. "It was a lovely gesture—"

"It wasn't a gesture."

"Well, it wasn't a proposal either."

His brows arched. His gaze raked over her features. Whatever he saw, it had his eyes warming and filling with a tenderness that made her ribcage feel far too small. "You're right." He shifted. "You deserve far better than that, Eloise."

"No, I didn't mean—"

He gripped her hands in his. "Your brother said your parents were telling everyone you were too far gone with grief to see visitors. They've covered for your absence."

The reminder of Pickington's death made her stomach turn.

"If we go back now, perhaps we could do this the right way."

Her lips parted with surprise and his gaze dipped, lingering on her mouth. He swallowed visibly. "I could court you the way you ought to be courted. I could speak with your father and—"

"No."

He blinked. "Pardon?"

She tore her hands from his as frustration mounted. "I cannot go back, Alex."

"Then come to the continent with me and—"

"I murdered your uncle."

Her words seemed to echo in the small room, and she felt certain the fire was mocking her with its incessant crackling and snapping.

He stared at her with wide eyes. "Pardon?"

"I-I—" She dropped her head into her hands. "Oh, I am a horrible person."

"You're not. Eloise..." He tugged her hands away from her face and held them in his. "You're not."

Tears welled in her eyes and her lips quivered. He seemed so very certain. As if he truly knew her. And for one very odd moment, she felt certain that he did. That maybe in some ways he knew her better than she knew herself.

"I did," she said with a sniffle. "He kissed me and it was awful and I pushed him."

"You pushed him," he repeated.

She nodded quickly. "I heard a thud and he groaned and..." She bit her lip to hold back a sob. "Don't you see? I killed him."

"Eloise. Sweetheart." He cupped her face in his hands. "Is that what you thought?"

"I...I..." She frowned. His lips were doing that thing again. "This isn't funny."

"No, it's definitely not. But El, you have to know." He leaned in closer. "You are not responsible for my uncle's death."

"But—"

"His heart gave out."

She blinked. "It did?"

"He'd been suffering from heart issues for years. The doctors told him to avoid rich foods and gatherings—"

"But he didn't," she whispered.

"He didn't. I'm no surgeon, but I don't believe a bump on the head could make his heart fail."

Her lips moved but no words came out. Relief was so overwhelming she slumped to the side and he caught her against his chest. "So I didn't...?"

His lips grazed her temple, his voice low and soothing. "You didn't."

They sat in silence as she let this sink in, only coming back to the moment when she felt his chest rise and fall quickly. Then she felt his breath against her ear and—

"Are you laughing at me?" She spun around to face him, his lips pressed together tight. "Don't you dare laugh."

"I would never," he said. As he laughed.

She glared, despite the fact that a laugh was bubbling up inside her. "A man is dead."

"A horrid man," he agreed.

"You still shouldn't be laughing at his passing," she shot back.

"I'm not laughing at his passing. I'm laughing that you believed yourself to be a murderer."

She narrowed her eyes. "It is not amusing."

"It is, rather." His chuckles were growing louder and it was getting harder and harder to maintain her serious expression.

She didn't particularly enjoy being laughed at, but she was still giddy with relief and she found herself sinking against him as the laughter she'd been fighting burst out of her. Helpless with it, she rested her head against his chest as he held her to him.

Swiping tears away, she struggled upright a moment later. "Well, that changes things then."

"It does, doesn't it?" he agreed. Shifting to face her, he asked, "Was that why you were so set on fleeing?"

She hesitated. "No. It didn't help matters, but aside from that, I couldn't go back. I just...couldn't."

He waited for her to continue but she took her time. She had the feeling that quite a bit rested on her response. Not just for him, but for her too.

It had been a long, tumultuous twenty-four hours. And while she desperately needed sleep, she found she needed to sort through her thoughts more.

"I wasn't thinking at all when I ran from Pickington's home."

He gave a snort of amusement along with a meaningful glance at her gown and slippers. "Clearly."

She smiled, seeing his teasing for what it was now. He was trying to cheer her up in his own odd way. He was always trying to cheer her up...when he wasn't driving her mad. Or confusing her senses.

One thing was clear. She wasn't apathetic about this man. He brought out reactions in her that were terrifying in their intensity. And she had a nagging, horrifying thought that now that she'd experienced those wild emotions, life would feel quite...empty once he was gone.

"You hadn't thought it through..." he prompted. His gaze was so studious. As if her every word mattered.

"Yes, but once I was gone, it was as if...as if I were suddenly free. And while that was frightening, it was also wonderful. And when you brought me back to my family home, I couldn't go back. It would be like trying to fit myself back into a gown I'd long since outgrown. I couldn't go backwards. It might have just been one night away, but it was enough."

"I understand that," he said.

"Do you?"

"Mmm." His expression grew serious. "There are some mistakes that cannot be undone. Some decisions that cannot be reversed. Words that cannot be unspoken and feelings that..." His gaze caught hers and held. "Feelings that once felt can't be denied."

She nodded, her heart beating far too fast. "Yes. Exactly."

"Eloise, there's something I need to say," he started slowly.

Her heart slammed against her chest at the seriousness in his gaze. His earlier words returned to her. His offer. So kind and so noble. "You do not have to offer for my hand."

The words tasted bitter. But it wouldn't be right to let him sacrifice himself because of her folly.

His brows came down. "I do not have to...or you do not want me to?"

Oh how her heart twisted and turned. How to answer that? Her mind's eye flooded with images of what it could be like if they were together.

She shoved the thoughts away. Because there would always be resentment and guilt between them if his reasons for proposing were anything less than heartfelt.

She placed a hand on his arm. "Alex, I...I don't want to trap you or force you to do the gallant thing."

He tried to argue, but she continued.

"I've been trapped, remember? I would not want that for you and you made it clear you don't wish to marry."

"Eloise—"

"What if..." She cut him off again, this time sitting bolt upright as she turned to face him fully. An idea was taking hold, one so reckless and dangerous it nearly made her gasp aloud.

He'd likely think so too, but she found herself saying it all the same.

"What if I were to come with you?"

His brows arched. "Come home with me? That's what I've been saying—"

"No. Not home. What if...what if I were to travel with you and...and..."

"And ruin your reputation for me?" He scowled. "I think not."

She knew he'd feel that way, but her heart was tumbling over itself. "But what if...Alex, you asked me what I want, and right now that is it. I want the family and the marriage, yes. But only when it is right." *And with you.* "But first... First I want an adventure. I want to travel and see the world and sort out who I am and where I'm meant to be."

He lifted a hand and caressed the soft skin of her cheek,

the tenderness of his touch matching the gentle affection in his tone. "Ah, love..."

She placed her hand over his, holding him to her. "I know how it sounds. But that way you would not be obligated to me. It would be my decision. My mistakes. And you won't have to marry because I know you don't wish to and—" She cut herself off abruptly at the seriousness in his eyes as he stared at her.

"You think I've lost my senses, don't you?" She aimed for teasing but her tone fell short. "I can see it."

"No, I understand your reasoning. But El, there's something I need to tell you."

The door to their little room flew open. Eloise gave a jolt and jerked back, ready to face the innkeeper or his wife.

Instead she faced Rodrick.

His face was flushed and his brow covered in sweat. He glared at her from the doorway. "There you are. Eloise, it's time to come home."

13

Alex's heart froze as Eloise shot to her feet with a gasp. "Rodrick?"

Then his heart took a sharp dive toward the ground as he watched Eloise's expression turn from gorgeously hopeful to...devastated.

Alex watched her stare open-mouthed at her brother, and he felt certain he could hear her thoughts loud as day. He saw the moment it registered...what he'd done.

She turned to him with hurt in her eyes and he felt it like a knife in his gut. No, not just hurt. Betrayal.

That look twisted the knife.

"El, I can explain," he started. His voice was low and Eloise ignored him.

Rodrick strode toward them. "Are you all right?" His gaze was raking over Eloise as he gripped her by the shoulders, taking in her disheveled state. "Are you hurt?"

She looked away from Alex. "No. No, I am not hurt."

She lied. Alex's insides felt charred. She was hurt. And he'd hurt her. "Eloise, I—"

"He sent for you, did he?" she asked her brother. Talking

about him as if he were not there. Her tone was light and calm, the voice he'd come to know in the ballroom. The sweet, dulcet tones she used to cover up that vast sea of emotions.

How had he ever found her simple or boring?

How had he ever thought her to be weak?

"El," Alex started again, but neither Eloise nor her brother was paying any attention to him.

"Eloise, how could you just run off like that?" Rodrick asked.

Alex flinched on her behalf because even he could hear the pain there. The true worry and hurt in his voice.

Her lips quivered. "I am sorry I worried you, Rodrick."

He gripped her by the shoulders again, but this time he pulled her to him for an embrace. Alex looked away from the emotional moment. It was not his to witness. But he heard her sob and Rodrick's soothing tones as he told her that all would be well.

Meanwhile, Alex bided his time, but with no degree of patience. His insides felt like they were being clawed apart by this need to explain himself to her, to make this right.

Had he sent for her brother? Yes. He'd told him precisely where they'd be and when. But he'd regretted it instantly. Even as he'd sent the note he'd known it was the wrong choice.

So why had he done it?

He stared into the fire. He'd been avoiding looking too closely at his motives all day and evening. But when he glanced over and caught Eloise peeking over at him, the hurt in her eyes plain as day...he couldn't avoid it any longer.

He'd been scared. He'd acted out of cowardice, plain and simple. She'd seen too much and cut too deep and made him feel things he'd never thought to experience. She'd reminded him of his childhood in all the worst ways and he'd let those old memories rule him.

I'm sorry. He tried to tell her as much with his eyes when her gaze met his. *That was before I realized just how strong you are, and just how brave.*

The innkeeper's wife came in, lightening the thick tension with her broad smile. "We've another brother to join us, eh?"

She gave Eloise a wink that had her blushing.

Eloise was achingly beautiful when her cheeks were flushed.

"If my room is ready, I should like to retire," Eloise said quietly.

"Of course, miss," the innkeeper's wife said. "I'll show you the way."

"Eloise," Rodrick said, his tone filled with warning.

Eloise smiled, but it didn't reach her eyes. "We'll talk in the morning. On our way home."

That silenced Rodrick, but it sent a sharp stab of panic straight through Alex. *Home.* She was going back...with Rodrick. "Eloise, wait," he said, striding toward her.

He stopped when she took two steps back, as if...as if afraid of him.

That ache in his chest was now a heavy weight that made breathing difficult.

"Allow me to explain," he said.

"No need," she said, her tone polite. "I understand."

"El—"

"I'm off to bed," she said, directing this to Rodrick, but making it abundantly clear that she had no desire to hear what Alex had to say.

They both watched her go, her head held high with pride.

His jaw felt like it might shatter when the door shut behind her, leaving him and Rodrick alone.

Rodrick sighed. "Thank you, Alex. I'm grateful to you."

Alex managed a grunt. His gaze was still fixed on the door as if she might return.

She wouldn't.

Perhaps in the morning she'd hear him out.

They'd both have clearer heads after they slept.

"I only wish you'd brought her back directly," Rodrick was saying, his arms crossed as he gave another weary sigh. "It will be difficult to explain her absence all this time, and if anyone discovers she was alone with you—"

"They won't," he said. "Not from me, at least. And we saw no one who would recognize us along the way."

"Good. That's good," Rodrick muttered. His gaze fixed on Alex with a new intensity. "But tell me, why did you risk it? Why did you bring her all this way? You could have just turned the carriage around and brought her home yourself."

Alex scoffed. "You think I ought to have dragged her back kicking and screaming?"

Rodrick shrugged helplessly. "I don't know, Alex. It's just..." He sighed again and Alex had the unpleasant sensation that he'd disappointed his friend. Rodrick met his gaze evenly. "She's just a scared young girl."

Alex was torn in two. On one hand, he felt thoroughly chastened by his longtime friend who he respected more than just about anyone.

But on the other hand...

Was he serious?

Alex peered at Rodrick. *Just a scared young girl.* Was that what he saw when he looked at Eloise? Because if so, he was mistaken. Eloise might have been scared, but she was no coward. And she might still be young, but she was no child.

But Rodrick was already turning away, scrubbing a hand over his eyes.

"You had quite the journey today," Alex said. "Why don't you take my room and get some sleep."

"What about you?" Rodrick asked.

"I'll be fine down here. I'm so tired I could sleep anywhere," he joked. "And besides, I'm sure Eloise would feel safer with her actual brother in the adjoining room."

Rodrick nodded. "Thank you." He paused and looked back on his way out. "And thank you again for taking care of her until I could retrieve her."

Alex nodded, his throat tight with emotions that he dreaded facing the moment Rodrick stepped out that door and left him alone.

"I know my family's chaos must have impeded your plans and—"

"Think nothing of it," Alex interrupted.

Rodrick nodded and walked out to find his room. Alex found himself staring after, bitter amusement coming out on a huff of air. Rodrick thought his sister had 'impeded his plans?'

Hardly.

Eloise had thoroughly upended his entire life.

He moved to the settee where only moments before he'd been holding Eloise in his arms, making promises and just beginning to take a step toward a future that was unknown and terrifying and...and potentially perfect.

He laid back, fully expecting his mind to run rampant, but sleep claimed him quick. The long day caught up with him and he sank into slumber, grateful for the reprieve. When he woke, however, he found that Rodrick and Eloise were not only up but were already preparing for their trip back to London.

"I'll check with the groom to see if the horses are ready," Rodrick told Eloise when Alex stumbled out of the dark back room and into the bright light of day that shone through the inn's large front windows.

Eloise was sitting primly by the front door as she smiled sweetly for her brother. So meek. So compliant.

So...wrong.

The moment Rodrick was out the door, Alex headed to her. He found himself drinking in the sight of her as if this would be the last time he saw her.

The thought was enough to make him stumble over his steps.

If she heard him coming, she ignored him. Her chin held high, her lips set in a firm line, she stared straight ahead.

She'd pinned her hair up neatly and had clearly washed the grime of travel off as much as possible, but it was still amazing to him how beautiful she looked even in her rumpled state.

"Eloise," he said when he drew near.

She met his gaze and came to stand. "Lord Wycliffe."

He frowned. So they were back to formalities, it seemed. "I'm sorry, El. You must know, I sent that messenger before..."

Before what? Before he'd realized how much she meant to him? Before she'd stolen his heart? It all sounded so implausible.

And she didn't wait to hear how he'd finish. "No apologies are necessary. I understand."

His brows hitched at her calm, sweet tone. That tone set his spine on edge and made his stomach turn with apprehension. This was not the strong woman he'd come to know.

This was not his Eloise.

"El," he started. "What we discussed last night—"

"Yes, it's clear to me now that you just needed to keep me here." Her smile came nowhere near her eyes. "Whatever it took to keep me pacified, right? Encourage my wild whims and fancies so I'd be here ready and waiting when my brother arrived, was that the plan?"

"No, that wasn't what—"

"I understand," she said. "I do."

She didn't. But he had no idea how to explain it to her. More than that, he wasn't sure he wanted to. This whole escapade had been lunacy from the start. Did he wish to take a wife? He hadn't his entire life. Was that really a decision he wanted to change? He might be the better of all her options, but was he what was best for her?

If she went back now and Rodrick and her family could keep her reputation intact, she could have her pick of suitors.

His gut heaved at the thought and his lips curved down in a glower. "If you go back, your parents will force you to marry another."

Her spine straightened. "No. They won't. I appreciate your concern, Lord Wycliffe, but you need not concern yourself with me and my future any longer."

He narrowed his eyes. She had a plan, that much was clear. A plan that did not involve him.

"I realized last night that you were right from the very beginning." Her gaze met his with such ferocity it made his lungs cease working for a moment.

"I was?"

"Yes." Anger and strength flared in her eyes, and she looked for all the world like some female warrior. "Running away from one's obligations and one's family is not just childish, it's cowardly." She tilted her chin up. "And I, for one, am tired of being afraid. I'll no longer act out of cowardice."

She might as well have planted a facer, the words hit that hard.

If she were a man he'd say she was calling him out. She wasn't trying to start a duel…yet she was questioning his honor. Nay, his strength of character.

"El, I—"

"I wish you well on your journey, my lord," she said, that cool tone back in place. "I hope you find all that you are looking for during your travels."

"Eloise." He reached out for her, but she stepped back quickly.

"El, are you ready?" Rodrick asked from the doorway.

She turned to her brother with a smile. "I am."

Alex watched her walk away. She never did look back, not so much as a glance.

I hope you find all you are looking for...

"I think...I already have," he said to the empty room.

14

𝓔loise was certain she'd be quite pleased if she never saw another carriage again.

They'd bought a simple travel gown on the journey home, but Eloise still felt as though she could bathe for a day and still be dirty.

She shifted uncomfortably as their carriage hit a rut that sent her and Rodrick bouncing.

"We'll be there soon," he said.

He'd said that several times already. As if by saying they were near would somehow make it so.

As if going 'home' were something she was eager to do.

They hadn't spoken much on this seemingly endless ride. But the closer they were to London and her parents, the more her newfound bravery began to falter.

She clasped her hands tightly in her lap.

"They will be happy to see you," Rodrick said. His tone was low and kind. He and Eloise were so much alike in so many ways. Neither had Charlotte's effervescent, some might say brash ways. Both were soft spoken.

And they both were exceptionally good at hiding the depth of their emotions.

"They'll be relieved, perhaps," she said. "I do not expect them to rejoice after what I've done."

Rodrick eyed her for a long moment, his gaze filled with concern. "Were you so very unhappy with Pickington?"

She assumed that was rhetorical, so she did not answer.

"Why did you not say so?"

"I tried not to think of it, honestly." She lifted a shoulder, grateful it was Rodrick she was confiding in. He, more than anyone, would understand. "I thought perhaps I could bear it if I just...did as I was told."

He nodded. "I wish you'd come to me, El."

She saw the hurt in his eyes and winced. "I'm sorry, Rodrick. I should have, but I didn't want to put you in a bad situation."

He leaned forward until his elbows rested on his knees. "You were worried about me? You were the one in danger, Eloise. I am your older brother, it is my responsibility to look after you."

She knew he meant well, but the words made her inwardly cringe. Truthfully, she was tired of being someone else's responsibility. She had no doubt that Alex had told himself the same. That he'd been looking after her in his own way. That he was doing what was best.

Her lungs could hardly draw in air and she leaned against the window. She let the wave of hurt wash over her.

She was done ignoring emotions and through pretending to be someone she was not. So she would not bury this hurt, but embrace it. Learn from it.

She'd been a fool to trust Alex, and hopelessly to believe that he might have felt some sort of connection between them. She'd been so sure it was there—a real, pure, strong bond—that she'd allowed herself to grow fanciful and romantic for the first time in her life.

But she was done with that now. Just like she was done being the family's puppet. She and Alex could agree on one thing, she supposed. It was time she looked after herself.

"You could have come to me," Rodrick said in a weary tone when she did not respond. "You could have come home."

"And then what?" she asked. "If I'd gone home, you know Mother and Father would only find a new replacement for Pickington. You might have tried to help, but to what end? You are not my legal guardian, and it would only end in you having to fight my battles for me." She leaned forward too, eager for him to understand. "I didn't want that."

She opted not to tell him that she'd also thought herself a murderer at the time. In hindsight, she was exasperated with herself for leaping to such a conclusion.

Her traitorous mind called up Alex's smile, the warm sound of his chuckle as he held her close.

She swallowed hard and looked down at her hands.

He'd been lying the entire time.

She'd tossed and turned for the better part of the night, and that was the conclusion she'd come to. He'd said whatever he'd had to just to keep her there at the inn until Rodrick arrived.

Maybe he'd worried she'd sneak off without him if he hadn't.

Oh, what did it matter why he'd done it?

What mattered was that he'd gone behind her back to send her home while selling her dreams of a future that would never be hers.

Humiliation burned in her belly.

Had he laughed? When she'd gone on about how she'd

travel with him, and when she'd talked about marrying for love?

All the while he'd known that he was sending her back to her parents. Back to being the good little girl who'd marry whoever they chose for her.

She straightened. "I can't go back there."

Rodrick's eyes widened. "El, you cannot—"

"No, no," she added quickly. "I am not saying that I wish to run away again. I have learned my lesson there."

She nearly flinched as she recalled her parting shot to Alex. She'd all but called him a coward for walking away from his responsibilities. But he would marry eventually, and he would do what was right. The difference was that he'd be able to choose his own spouse, and he could do it whenever he chose.

She drew in a deep breath. "I will not run away again."

Rodrick's shoulders slumped with relief.

"But I do not want to go back home either. I will speak to Mother and Father. I will explain why I left and I will suffer their censure but...I cannot go back to being their dutiful daughter."

He nodded slowly. "Do you want to come live with me?"

Eloise thought it over. It wasn't a bad idea, though he was to marry Franny in a few months' time and she did not wish to intrude on the newlyweds. Plus, it might cause undue talk among the *ton*—assuming she was not already ruined. But Rodrick assured her that no one but their immediate family knew that she'd left.

"Where were you planning to go?" Rodrick asked, curiosity in his features as he studied her as if seeing her for the first time. "When you ran off, I mean."

"To see Charlotte," she admitted.

"Ah," he said. "And instead you found yourself with Lord Wycliffe."

THE MISPLACED MISS ELOISE

A muscle in her jaw twitched at the mention of Alex. She did not miss the questions in his warm brown eyes...

But she had no inclination to answer them.

"It was not his fault," she said. Though she suspected Rodrick knew as much. Still, no matter how much Alex might have hurt her feelings, he was Rodrick's dear friend and she'd hate to come between them.

"Perhaps we can still find a way for you to spend time abroad with Charlotte," Rodrick said.

Her brows arched. "Truly?"

He smiled. "Did I not tell you I was on your side, El? I will talk to Mother and Father about giving you time before there is any further talk of marriage."

Her throat grew tight. "Thank you."

His smile grew, making his eyes crinkle at the corners. "Perhaps I'll try to make them believe that Charlotte would be a good influence on you."

Eloise burst out laughing and Rodrick grinned.

"Well, she is a married lady now," Rodrick teased.

Eloise shook her head. "Oh, how the tides have turned. Charlotte is the dutiful daughter who married well and I am..." She winced. "Trouble."

But even while wincing she smiled.

She was trouble. She rather liked the sound of that.

"I think I have an idea," Rodrick said suddenly.

She arched her brows. "I'm all ears."

"With Charlotte touring the continent, her room should be available at Miss Farthington's Finishing school..."

"The School of Charm?" Hope flickered in her chest. She'd spent quite of bit of time there over the last few months, first to visit Charlotte and then to spend time with Charlotte's friend Mary, who'd become a friend to her as well.

Mary was a dear, and everyone knew Miss Farthington

had been tainted by a scandal of her own when her engagement came to an end. She knew little of Miss Lydia, the other girl currently living at the school's townhome, but she seemed a sweet, shy young thing.

Most of all, she could live there without causing undue gossip, and it would give her some space from her parents.

"Yes. Yes, that would be wonderful," she said.

"Then it is decided. We'll go home first." He winced in sympathy. "I'm afraid it's unavoidable."

She tipped her chin in acknowledgment. She wasn't exactly looking forward to this encounter but she agreed that it could not be put off.

"And I will send word to Miss Farthington," he continued.

She nodded, breathing deeply for the first time since they'd left Alex behind. This was it. The first step in her new life.

A life without Alex.

Which was fine. Obviously. She'd only known him a short while. And while he might have hurt her...badly, she couldn't possibly have such strong feelings for him that he could affect her for long.

She told herself that multiple times over the last leg of their journey. The reminder was necessary because her silly mind kept calling up memories of him as if...oh drat.

As if she already missed him.

She wasn't allowed to miss a man she barely knew.

But neither her mind nor her heart seemed to be listening to reason.

By the time they arrived home, Eloise was almost too tired and dispirited to be anxious over the reception she'd receive.

And what she got was...loud. There was much shouting. Even more wringing of hands. But Eloise was pleasantly surprised that their relief at having her home seemed to outweigh their anger at what she'd done.

The hardest part was speaking her mind, but she did it. "Mother, Father," she said when the commotion had settled. "I am truly sorry for running away."

"You've learned your lesson at least," her father had grumbled.

"I've learned that it was foolish to run rather than confront you both with my feelings," she said.

They exchanged a look.

"And what are your *feelings*?" her father asked.

It was difficult to ignore her father's snide tone, but she saw through it. He wasn't as cold and heartless as Charlotte always made him out to be. Neither was their mother. They'd just become so very good at pushing their emotions deep down beneath the surface that it was easy to wonder if they had any at all.

But they did. Of course they did. They were human, after all.

And with that reminder, she laid her heart bare. "I know that I must marry," she said. "But I will not marry a man I despise."

"Lord Pickington was a good choice—"

"For you," Eloise interrupted her mother as gently as she was able. "Not for me."

It took quite a bit of talking, and more than a little pleading, but by the end of it all an agreement had been reached.

15

*A*lex rocked on his heels, his arms crossed over his chest as he studied the hull of the ship before him.

It was time to make a decision.

A foghorn sounded and shouts could be heard from the sailors preparing the ship for its voyage.

Truthfully, it was well past time. He'd been dallying here on the dock all morning. The weather had cleared, the ship was set to sail...

But Alex couldn't quite bring himself to be on it.

The ship began to move, sailing away from the dock.

Alex sighed. Oh, all right, perhaps it was time to admit that he'd already made his decision. That his decision had been made for him the moment he'd watched Eloise walk out of the inn.

He had to go after her. There was no other way. He'd had the most alarming notion that when she'd left, she'd taken a part of him with her.

Now the only option was to go after her to get it back.

Still, he'd lingered. Some part of him needed to feel as if he was actually making the decision with reason and logic.

But of course that wasn't the case.

His heart had decided and it wouldn't be budged. But even so, he'd stood here, watching the sun rise overhead and listening to the waves pounding against the shore.

He couldn't bring himself to get on the ship, but he wasn't certain he was ready to turn back and head to London either.

Why not?

He frowned out at the water as if the answers could be found there. They couldn't. Instead, his mind seemed to mimic the swirling, churning waves, battering about like he was in the midst of his own personal storm.

On one hand, he wanted her.

Badly.

Not just physically, although he'd be lying to himself if he said he wasn't drawn to her beauty. But it was her spirit, her heart, her kindness and her strength that made his heart ache whenever he thought of her.

It was the way he felt around her, as though he'd found the place where he belonged...

And that place was a person.

He longed to kiss her, to hold her in his arms. He'd happily attend the most tedious society events for the chance to take her into his arms for another waltz. But...

Was wanting Eloise enough? Because if his parents had taught him anything, it was that selfishness could destroy a person. His father had wanted his mother, and where had that gotten them?

He was not his father, no—and thank heavens for that. But he'd lived a solitary life. He didn't know how to be a good friend, let alone a decent husband.

He'd already let her down once. He'd betrayed her trust out of cowardice and fear. What was to say he would not do it again?

Whatever guidance from above that hadn't let him step

foot on that ship, it was at play again when he found himself walking away from the shore, back to the inn.

He made the arrangements for travel without thinking too far ahead.

He could not stay here staring out at the sea for eternity. But he wasn't quite sure he was ready to go back to London either. Eloise didn't want him chasing after her. And truthfully, he felt a swell of pride every time he thought of her set chin and that glitter of defiance in her eyes as she'd stood up to him.

She was going home to face her demons...and her parents.

And perhaps it was time that he did the same.

The travel to his family's country estate felt longer than the journey to the shore. But perhaps that was because he didn't have Eloise there with him.

The sprawling manor seemed to creep out of the fog as his carriage drew near. And just like at the shoreline, he found himself stopping to stare for long moments, as if all the answers could be found by staring at the home that had housed him during his miserable childhood.

When he went inside, he startled the poor housekeeper with the suddenness of his arrival, but she hurried into action, readying the estate for him.

"I won't be staying long," he said.

Hopefully.

Just long enough to come to grips with his past so that he might face the future.

As Alex settled on the settee in front of a roaring fire, he tried desperately not to think of the two other occasions when he'd sat before a fire just like this one with a darling, feisty, surprising little angel at his side.

And now he found himself sharing the room with ghosts.

Oh, he did not truly believe in spirits and specters, but he was certain he could feel them all the same. Memories seemed to fill every wretched corner of this old, drafty house.

Not a home. Never a home.

Just a residence. The place where he'd learned to fear his father's harsh hand and to pity his poor mother. His every memory of her was dim and hazy. Not because he did not remember, but because she'd been such a tepid presence in this house.

It was as though she'd tried to disappear long before she actually took her life.

As one night stretched into two, and Alex's brief visit to his ancestral home became a fortnight's stay, he was forced to confront the fact that it wasn't just pity he'd felt for his mother.

It was anger, too.

Anger that she hadn't protected him. That she hadn't tried. Now as an adult, he could see it more clearly. And with enough time spent lingering in the salon and the drawing room, taking his place behind the desk that was once his father's and airing out his mother's quarters, he rid the house of its ghosts.

He rid himself of their shackles.

His mother might have loved him, but she hadn't been able to protect him any more than she'd been able to protect herself. And it was time to forgive her for that. To pity her, yes, but to give her memory the love and understanding that he was capable of now that he was grown.

And his father...

Well, his father did not deserve anything from him. Not his understanding, and certainly not his love.

But he also didn't deserve to have power over Alex any longer.

He'd had enough of that during his lifetime.

Time and reflection helped Alex to slowly but surely

remove the shackles he'd been wearing without even realizing it.

For Eloise had been right. He'd been running from his past, just as she'd been. And if he were to earn her trust and be worthy of her love, it was time to show the same strength she had.

It was time to stop running.

Through it all, she was front and center in his mind's eye. And nearly every minute of every day he found himself wondering what she was doing and how she fared.

Had she stood up to her parents? Of course she had. But how had they responded?

Did she need him?

Was she even now on the run again?

But deep down he knew better. Eloise was done running. And if she could face her parents, then surely he could face his.

"Well, here I am," he said one night as he sat alone with his memories and a drink in hand. "Facing the past. You have no power over me any longer. I will not be the cruel man my father became. And I've fallen in love with a woman who wouldn't let herself or her child be treated poorly. Eloise is strong, Mother. You'd like her."

And he was absolutely losing his mind because he was sitting here talking to his deceased mother.

"Perhaps it's time," he said, to no one in particular.

A smile tugged at his lips for the first time in what felt like ages. It was time. He was ready to face Eloise. To tell her all he'd realized, and to woo her the way she deserved.

If she'd have him.

The thought had his smile fading, but his jaw set with determination.

Would she send him away? Maybe. But if she did, he

knew what he'd do. He'd come back. Again and again, if need be.

He'd failed her once by betraying her trust. He wouldn't fail her again. And whether she realized it or not—whether she wanted to admit it or not—he was the man for her.

He had to be. Because she was the woman of his heart.

The next morning he had his servants get preparations underway for the far shorter journey back to London.

He'd done what he'd come here to do, and he'd made his peace. Now it was time to claim his bride.

"There's a solicitor here to see you, my lord," the housekeeper said, hovering in his study doorway with a worried frown.

"Send him in."

Alex rose when the silver-haired gentleman arrived.

"Ah, Lord Wycliffe, I am glad I found you at home," the older man said. Mr. Shipman his name was, and he wasted no time in getting to the point.

"I've come with sad tidings, I'm afraid." The older man smiled cryptically. "Though you might view it as a boon."

Alex arched his brows. "Is that so?" He glanced at the clock on the mantel. "Well, I'll admit I am intrigued, Mr. Shipman. But if we could make this brief, I'd appreciate it." He smiled. "You see, I have the most important business of my life to attend to. And she's waiting for me in London."

Waiting for you? That's a stretch.

But she *was* waiting for him, Alex decided. He refused to entertain the possibility that she would choose another. She had to love him back, because a future without Eloise was impossible to consider.

So yes, she was waiting for him.

She just didn't know it yet.

16

Eloise had settled into a routine at the School of Charm and this evening had come to be the norm. Her friend Mary was out at the theater with her fiancé, but Eloise and her new friend Lydia were seated before the fire.

Lydia was silent beside her, curled up on an armchair with her head buried in a book, as usual. Were Mary here, she would have had her head buried in a book as well, though she preferred textbooks and science journals.

Meanwhile, Eloise had just finished writing a response to Charlotte's last letter and had turned her attention to the note she'd received via messenger from her mother.

While her parents hadn't relished the idea of her leaving their home, they relented in the end. They also acquiesced to her request that all talk of matrimony be temporarily put to the side.

Though this was a far more tentative arrangement.

She pursed her lips as she eyed the invitation in her hands.

"Is everything all right?" Miss Farthington asked.

The headmistress sat beside her, and Eloise smiled ruefully as she held up the missive. "A note from my mother."

"Ah." Miss Farthington's expression was knowing. Likely because she did know. She and Eloise had talked a great deal since she'd taken up residence in Charlotte's old room, and it had become instantly clear that they had much in common.

Including 'good' matches that had ended abysmally. Though Miss Farthington's fiancé had not died on the eve of her wedding. That might have been too much of a coincidence.

But she did know what it was to go from having one's life plotted out like an already written novel to having that book burnt in a fire with not so much as a scrap of parchment left to say where the character was meant to go.

Not that Eloise was complaining. She welcomed this newfound unknown future. Even if it was mildly terrifying.

"She wishes for me to attend a small dinner party she's hosting," Eloise explained as she returned her gaze to the missive in hand.

"Will you attend?" Miss Farthington asked.

Eloise hitched her lips to the side as she considered. "My mother has not asked much of me since my return."

Miss Farthington nodded. "This is true."

In fact, in many ways her mother seemed to be trying to mend their relationship. Eloise suspected neither of her parents had truly understood just how much their high-handed ways had affected their daughters. But it seemed Eloise's actions had opened their eyes.

"But then again," Eloise added slowly. "I have a feeling my mother will have invited new potential suitors to this soiree."

Miss Farthington laughed. "It is highly possible."

Eloise gave her new friend a wry grin. Miss Farthington had joined in on enough of her mother's visits to know the gist of it. While she did seem to be trying to change, she was

THE MISPLACED MISS ELOISE

still a marriage-minded mother at heart. And she wanted to ensure that Eloise made a good match and was well taken care of.

Though at least now she seemed to take Eloise's feelings into consideration as well.

"Would that be so terrible?" Miss Farthington asked. "To meet new eligible gentlemen?"

Lydia lifted her head, her bright green eyes fixed on her with blatant curiosity that had Eloise biting her lip.

Lydia was quiet. Shy to the extreme. The sweet redhead tended to blush if anyone looked at her directly. But from the moment Eloise had arrived, she and Lydia had been the dearest of friends.

Eloise suspected it was because their natures were so very complimentary. Perhaps it was because Eloise was soft spoken by nature and prone to smiles, but even Miss Farthington had commented that Lydia seemed more at ease around Eloise than anyone else. And for Eloise's part, Lydia's quiet nature was like a balm after living with her overbearing parents. She was so easy to be around that they often spent hours in the same space, talking some but mostly enjoying the easy companionship.

On those times when Eloise had needed a listening ear and a shoulder to cry on, Lydia had been there for her.

And so now, Lydia likely understood why Eloise hesitated to answer.

"I know I cannot avoid matrimony forever," Eloise said slowly. "And I do not wish to."

She hesitated again, and Miss Farthington patted her hand. "Then perhaps it would not be so terrible to go to this soiree, even if you find yourself the center of much attention."

Eloise blushed and nodded, but she shared a look with Lydia whose expression was tight with concern.

"I suppose you're right, it's just..." She swallowed hard. She hadn't wanted Miss Farthington to know the whole tale of her adventure with Alex. Not because she would judge or gossip, but because she did not wish to horrify the genteel earl's daughter. Nor did she wish to put her in a bad spot with her parents.

It was one thing to ask Lydia to keep her secrets, but Miss Farthington had an obligation to her parents first and foremost.

And so now, she hedged with her answer. "I suppose it would not be so terrible."

And it wouldn't have been. If there wasn't already one very particular man who had infiltrated her thoughts and filled her dreams.

It was irritating, truly, the way he'd somehow managed to take up so much space in her heart and her mind when they'd only known one another for such a short while.

She'd all but forgotten what Lord Pickington looked like days after he'd passed, but more than a fortnight later and she could still remember with perfect accuracy the way Alex's mouth creased at the corners when he smiled and the exact shade of his eyes when he teased her.

Infuriating man. Whatever he'd done to her, it was exhausting and annoying and...

And she feared it was permanent.

The thought had her heart sinking. He was gone. Probably in France right about now, charming some poor, unsuspecting young mademoiselle with his blunt manners and that mesmerizing twitch of his lips.

He was gone, and that was that. It was for the best.

She took a deep breath and forced a smile. "Perhaps you're right. Maybe it is time for me to move on."

Miss Farthington likely thought she meant from Pickington and her engagement. But a sympathetic little grimace from Lydia said that she, at least, knew to whom she referred.

It was time to rid her mind of the dashing viscount who had no desire to marry. It was time to focus on her own future.

"Yes," she said with a sharp nod. "I shall go. My mother has invited you both and Mary, as well." She arched her brows in question.

"I'm afraid Mary and I have already committed to having dinner with Lord Paul's family tomorrow," Miss Farthington said. Her eyes glinted with mischief. "But Miss Lydia is free..."

Lydia shifted, drawing backwards as if she could sink into the cushions of her chair.

Eloise smiled at her new friend. "Oh, I do hope you will come." It was cruel of her, she knew it, but she still added, "I could use your support."

Lydia's expression grew pained.

Miss Farthington smiled kindly. "No one will force you, dear, you know that."

"Of course not," Eloise added. "But the more I get to know you, the more certain I am that you are ready to shed this paralyzing shyness of yours."

Lydia arched her brows, her cheeks pink as if this embarrassed her. "Do you really think so?"

"I do," Eloise said. "And do you know why?"

Lydia shook her head.

Eloise leaned forward to squeeze her hand. "Because there is a great big world out there, and it is filled with wonderful people and places and music and laughter. And you deserve to experience it all."

Lydia's smile grew and she laughed softly. "All right. You win." With a feigned huff of irritation, she added, "You certainly know how to get your way when you wish, don't you?"

"I suppose perhaps I take after my mother in that sense," Eloise agreed with a laugh. "But I only want what's in your best interest."

She flinched. Oh dear. Now she truly did sound like her mother.

She tried again. "But only if it's what you want."

Both ladies were laughing at her now.

"Darling Eloise, you only ever have the best of intentions," Lydia said. "And you're right, of course." Her eyes grew distant. "There is much that I would like to see and experience." She gave a definitive nod. "I will go to the dinner party with you tomorrow night. I cannot promise I will speak to anyone, but it will be a step forward."

Eloise grinned and shared a triumphant look with Miss Farthington.

She wasn't sure Lydia realized just how far she'd come already. Even that little speech she just gave was far more than she'd ever spoken when she'd first arrived here at the school.

"Wonderful," Eloise said. Her belly twisted and turned with nerves.

It was one thing to resist her parents' expectations and highhandedness while living in another residence. But her heart fluttered with nerves the next day as she prepared herself to see her parents and find out who they were trying to match her with this time.

Her mind called up an image of a grim face and teasing eyes.

She scowled at her reflection as a maid pinned her hair up.

Dratted Alex and his ridiculously handsome face. Why couldn't she stop thinking of him?

He had no place in her thoughts tonight, not when she had no doubt she was on her way to meeting new suitors. Hopefully younger than Pickington. And with more hair.

She nibbled on her lip as she and Lydia climbed into the carriage that her father had sent for them. She had a nagging fear that all had been going too well between her and her parents since her return.

"What if I am walking into a trap?" she asked Lydia.

Her friend winced sympathetically as she reached for her hand, but she didn't try to protest. She'd heard enough between Charlotte and Eloise to know just how single minded her parents could be when it came to making a good match.

"I met my deceased fiancé's brother, you know," she told Lydia. "The new Pickington lives up north, but he came to visit not long after our engagement was announced."

"And?" Lydia asked, fear in her eyes on Eloise's behalf.

"He's worse," she said with a shake of her head. "It's hard to imagine, but he was even worse."

"Surely your parents would not try and make a match with him after what happened," Lydia said.

Eloise swallowed hard. Hopefully not. But right now she was having second thoughts about this brave plan of hers to face her family and her fate head on.

Surely life on the run would have been better.

Her heart twisted at the memory of a disheveled Alex with that fiery light in his eyes and the stubble on his jaw...

She swallowed hard. He was likely enjoying that life on the run right now. And she was here. Ready to meet more gentlemen who'd see her as a prized possession at best.

She let out a long harsh exhale. Nonsense. She'd changed. And while her parents might be difficult, they'd changed too.

She thought.

She hoped.

"We're here," Lydia whispered as the carriage drew to a stop.

For a moment, as the two girls gripped hands, Eloise wasn't sure which of them was more terrified.

Eloise let out another sharp exhale. "Right. Let's do this, shall we? Together."

"Together," Lydia echoed weakly.

And together they headed out of the carriage and into the brightly lit entryway of her family home. The house was already alive with laughter and music.

"Ah, there she is now," her father's voice boomed. "We were just talking about you."

Eloise's smile felt brittle.

"I thought you said this was going to be an intimate dinner party," Lydia hissed at her side.

"Lydia, this *is* intimate...for my mother." She forced a wider smile as she took Lydia's arm. "Come. Let us be brave."

She spotted Rodrick and his fiancée, as well as Franny's parents, and several of her brother's friends.

"Look, there's Rodrick," Eloise said.

Lydia had grown somewhat accustomed to her brother these past few weeks.

"If I am otherwise engaged for some reason, go seek him out." Eloise patted Lydia's hand. "He will ensure no one pesters you too much."

Lydia nodded, her face pale. "All right."

"As for me..." Eloise started.

Her mother spotted her and was coming straight toward her.

Eloise never did get to finish.

"Eloise, darling, you look lovely," her mother said, kissing her cheeks in greeting. "I have wonderful news."

Eloise's stomach dropped. "Oh yes?"

Her mother leaned in with a conspiratorial whisper. "We

THE MISPLACED MISS ELOISE

have a special guest dining with us tonight. He was most interested in meeting you."

"Was he?" Her voice sounded shrill.

She couldn't do this. It wasn't right. All she could think of was Alex.

Which was ridiculous.

He'd left.

He'd left her.

He'd sent her back home and had sought out a future without her. She had to let him go. She'd been wrong about him. That connection she'd thought they shared—she'd been naive and idiotic and...

And it was no use.

No amount of telling herself so could make her feel any different. What was worse, she wasn't sure if what she was feeling was dread at meeting some gentleman her parents chose...or guilt at meeting another man at all.

Why did it feel like she'd be betraying Alex if she were to entertain another gentleman?

It made no sense at all.

But try explaining that to her heart.

"Ah, this must be him now," her mother said when there was a commotion at the door. "Right on time."

"Mother, I..."

But her mother was already heading toward the doorway to the ballroom where the butler had paused to announce the new guest and Eloise felt her limbs go cold as the new arrival was announced.

"Lord Pickington," his voice boomed.

Her stomach turned, her heart twisted, and then...

Then the floor gave out beneath her because the new guest filled the doorway and it was him. She'd have recognized that jawline anywhere, even if it wasn't covered in stubble. And his eyes...oh those eyes.

147

They fixed on her with that glint of amusement and teasing that was so uniquely him.

The ground beneath her quivered.

"Alex?" she managed.

And then the room went dark as she fell.

17

*A*lex was the first to reach her side.
Likely because he'd seen what was about to happen.

"Eloise," he said, his heart tripping as he knelt beside her, ignoring the shocked outbursts of the other guests.

"El?" Rodrick was next to him, his mother on his other side.

"I'll fetch the smelling salts," she said.

Rodrick glared over at Alex. "What have you done?"

"Er..." Alex grimaced, but his attention was fixed on the lovely blonde before him.

The lovely *unconscious* blonde. But even as they stared, she began to stir, and Alex felt a surge of relief and tenderness so overwhelming it took everything in him not to pull her up and into his arms.

"She needs air," he said to Rodrick. "Where can I take her?"

"I'll take her," Rodrick snapped.

Alex's hands clenched into fists. Of course. It wasn't his

right...yet. But every instinct in his body clamored to shout that she was his to protect.

"Let us through," Rodrick said to the gathered crowd as he scooped Eloise into his arms and hoisted her up.

Alex saw Rodrick's fiancée and a redhead hovering nearby with matching looks of concern.

"She's all right," he told the crowd at large, hoping to assuage their concern and perhaps ease their curiosity. "She just had a shock, that's all."

"That's all?" Rodrick muttered under his breath. "She took one look at you and fainted." He glared at Alex. "Eloise never faints."

"So she says," Alex murmured.

Rodrick set her gently on a settee in a small parlor near the back of the house. The sound of chatter could be heard, but the crowd felt far away.

Eloise stirred again, her eyes fluttering open. Rodrick didn't seem to notice, but when her bright blue eyes landed on him, Alex felt his heart explode with emotion.

Terror that she would send him away, relief that she was all right, but mostly love. Pure, sweet, overwhelming affection for this woman who'd managed to turn his life upside down in the course of one full day.

"What did you do?" Rodrick asked again. "When you came back here and asked for an invitation..." Rodrick's eyes narrowed with suspicion. "Alex, what have you done?"

"It's all right, Rodrick." Eloise was struggling to sit upright, but she froze with a mutinous glare when Alex tried to help her.

Rodrick watched them both closely. "What exactly is going on here? What happened between you two?"

But before they could answer, Eloise's mother entered, her father not far behind.

"Eloise, are you all right?" Her father sounded genuinely concerned.

"I'm fine," she whispered.

Anyone could see she was not. But right now what aggravated Alex the most was that she would not meet his gaze. He had no way of knowing how she felt about his sudden arrival.

Though, if her swooning were anything to go by, perhaps surprising her tonight had not been the best idea.

"I did not eat enough today, that's all," Eloise was saying.

Her mother pursed her lips. "I'll tell the cook to prepare you something right away. It will not do for you to faint face first in the soup."

"No, indeed." Her father was glancing toward the door. "I'll assure our guests that you are all right." He turned to Alex with an ingratiating smile. "Lord Pickington, I do hope you'll forgive this little..." He glanced at Eloise with a wince of chagrin. "Incident."

Alex's teeth clenched as Eloise blushed.

It could not be more clear what was going on here. Rodrick's father had never taken much interest in him before. But now that he was the new Earl of Pickington he was a guest of honor.

Not only that, but her mother was casting furtive, eager glances between him and Eloise. "My lord, you'd mentioned that you were hoping to become acquainted with my daughter this evening."

Her gaze snapped up at that and he found himself staring straight into her eyes. They blazed with an angry fire.

His jaw twitched. He couldn't blame her. But none of this was going as it ought. He'd meant for this to be a pleasant surprise. A grand gesture, as it were.

But her parents were making it seem all wrong.

"Lord Pickington," Eloise murmured softly...but loudly enough for him to hear.

"Yes," he said, keeping his tone aloof for her parents' sake. He'd spoken to Rodrick and knew that he'd been left out of the story of Eloise's adventure.

No one, least of all Eloise, had wanted to be forced into a marriage.

He, Eloise, and Rodrick might be well aware of the fact that they'd gotten to know one another over the course of that ill-fated trip, but as far as her parents were concerned, they were only now becoming acquainted.

"It was a surprise to me as well," he said to Eloise now, holding her gaze evenly. "You see, I returned home to discover that your fiancé's younger brother had passed away as well."

Her eyes popped open. "No."

He grimaced. "I'm afraid so. It was a carriage accident, you see."

"So..." She trailed off with a frown. "So, you are now the new Lord Pickington."

He held his arms out wide. "It would seem so."

She blinked at him.

"Believe me, no one was more shocked than I was," he said.

Her lips worked and her gaze flickered to her parents. He could all but see her trying to figure out how much they knew and what she could safely say. Eloise cleared her throat. "When you arrived home," she repeated. "I thought you told me...er, at my wedding celebration you mentioned that you would be traveling to the continent."

His heart did a leap as hope flared. This was it, what he'd come to say.

Just...not in front of her entire family. "There was a change of plans."

"Oh yes?" she breathed.

Was he imagining things or was that hope in her eyes too?

"Rather, it was a change of heart," he said.

She pressed her lips together.

"I realized that I'd left rather urgent business behind."

Urgent business. He inwardly winced. Not the most romantic turn of phrase, but he had to believe she'd understand.

Her eyes narrowed. "Indeed."

Was that good or bad? He could not say. Impatience made his voice brusque as he spoke to her parents. "Do forgive me, but I have another obligation this evening." He glanced pointedly toward the door. "I have heard so much about your daughter, and considering her relationship with my uncle..."

Her mother's gaze brightened.

"Oh, of course," she said. The woman was quick, he'd give her that. Quick...and very eager to see her daughter become the countess she was meant to be.

He tried not to notice the way Eloise was now glaring at him. She was quick too, of course. She knew precisely what game he was playing.

But if it meant having a moment of relative privacy, he'd do whatever it took.

"We shall be just outside with our guests," her father said. He arched a brow at Rodrick.

Rodrick, in turn, was eyeing Alex warily. "I shall stay here and act as chaperone."

Perfect. That was precisely what they'd agreed upon earlier. Though...

He did feel rather guilty now. Clearly Rodrick was suspicious, and with good reason. He ought to be because Alex had every intention of kissing Eloise and sweeping her off her feet.

If she didn't murder him first.

With her parents gone, the room grew tense and silent. Rodrick cleared his throat. Out of the corner of his eye, Alex could see him looking back and forth between them.

"Rodrick, may I please speak with Eloise privately?"

Rodrick looked to Eloise who nodded.

Alex's heart resumed beating with that one little nod. There was hope for him yet.

"I'll be right over here," Rodrick said, moving to the far corner of the room and looking out through the glass panes of the French doors leading to a veranda.

Eloise went to stand but he held out a hand to stop her.

"Please," he said. "Your brother will never forgive me if I cause you to faint again."

She pursed her lips in irritation.

"Ah, I forgot," he said. He couldn't help the teasing tone. "You never faint."

She pressed her lips together but not before he caught a flicker of amusement.

She remembered that first night together, at least. He supposed that was something.

Or it wasn't and he was just in dire need of reassurance wherever he could find it.

"What are you doing here?" she asked. "And how did I not know you were the new earl?"

She cast that last question in Rodrick's direction and Alex saw his friend stiffen.

"My fault, I'm afraid," Alex said quickly. "I asked your brother to keep my presence in London a secret until I had a chance to talk to you."

"Why?" she asked.

Her face was still pale but there was a wariness in her eyes that made his heart ache.

"Because I was afraid you would refuse to see me if you knew I was coming," he said bluntly.

She visibly swallowed but didn't protest. "Would you blame me?"

He moved until he was beside her and went down on his knees so their faces were level. "Not at all. I should have told you that I'd sent for your brother," he said.

"You shouldn't have sent for him in the first place," she said.

He didn't argue.

She looked away with a shake of her head. "Or maybe you should have. I don't know. Heaven knows I didn't handle myself well—"

"On the contrary," he said. "I found you to be quite remarkable."

She cast him a sidelong glance as if trying to determine if he were serious.

"It's not many women who would climb into a strange man's trunk."

Her lips twitched ever so slightly before she squelched the smile. "Well, when you put it like that, it's no wonder you called for reinforcements. I must have seemed quite mad."

"Not mad," he said. "Just...desperate."

She nodded, her gaze pained. "I suppose I was."

"And now?" He reached for her hand and tried not to flinch when she pulled away from his grip. He forced a smile. "Did you introduce your family to the new and improved Eloise?"

She lifted a shoulder. "I tried. I'm not sure how much good it will do in the long run." She worried her lower lip as her fingers fidgeted next to his on the settee. "They have promised to take my wishes into consideration." Her eyes narrowed. "But that is not to say that they will not try and pressure me into something if they believe it to be in everyone's best interests."

"Ah, yes." He cleared his throat. She was referring to the

subtle hint he'd made before. "You must know I would never use my new position of power to force your hand."

She arched a brow. "Must I?"

That hurt. It hurt far more than he would have expected.

She looked away. "But of course, you wouldn't do that, would you? You made it clear that you have no desire to marry. And certainly not to me."

"My, what a sharp memory you have."

She glanced back at his teasing tone.

"First of all, I hardly knew you when I said that."

"You hardly know me now."

"True," he said. "And that is precisely why I came back. It is what I'd hoped to remedy."

She blinked rapidly. "I don't understand."

His heart was on a silver platter, and she had no idea. "I came back because I realized... That is... I want to court you, Eloise."

Her stare was intent but blank.

"The moment you were gone... No, before that. I knew that you'd changed everything. I didn't want to let you go. But I also knew you deserved better."

She wet her lips. "What are you saying?"

"I'm saying..." He reached for her hands again and this time she didn't pull away. "I'm saying, I love you, Eloise. I've never met anyone like you. I've never felt this connection to anyone before, and I...I want to court you. Properly."

The silence that stretched in the wake of his speech was the longest of his life. And then finally she opened her mouth and she...

She ran away.

18

*E*loise had a problem.
  This much was clear.
Her lungs couldn't get enough air as Alex's voice filled her mind and made her heart feel dangerously close to shattering.

She didn't exactly intend to run. But the tension in the room was unbearable, the look in his eyes so expectant, and her mind was a complete and utter blank.

Add to that the way her heart was racing and her lungs refusing to work and...

And she was up and rushing toward the veranda doors before so much as a squeak could escape, let alone some polite excuse. She was dimly aware of Rodrick calling her name as she passed but then she was out in the cold night air and finally, finally she could breathe.

And cry.

Apparently crying was in order as well, though for the life of her she couldn't say why.

From out here she could hear the sounds of revelry from

the drawing room farther down. Lydia would be worrying about her, she knew.

Her parents were likely waiting with bated breath to know what had transpired.

Alex was Lord Pickington.

Alex was here.

Alex was in love with her.

She shook her head. No. Still didn't quite make sense. It was all too much and too quickly. She'd been trying so hard these past weeks to move on from the feelings he'd stirred in her on their journey. She'd ruthlessly squashed thoughts of him every time they arose and had done her very best to ignore the swell of feelings that came with them.

But now he was here, and there was no avoiding it.

She heard the door open behind her and braced for Alex's low voice, and the warm, welcoming scent of him. She waited for another crushing wave of homesickness to overwhelm her like it had the moment she'd first caught sight of him.

How ridiculous to be homesick for a man she'd only just met.

But it was Rodrick's voice she heard behind her.

"El?" His footsteps drew closer. "Are you all right?"

She turned to him with teary eyes. "I have certainly developed a flair for the dramatic, haven't I?"

His smile was indulgent, his gaze filled with concern. "Charlotte will be most pleased."

They shared a rueful chuckle but hers ended with a choked sob.

"Oh, what am I to do, Rodrick?" She swiped at her cheeks. "I hardly recognize myself any longer."

"Is that so bad?" he asked, leaning against the balustrade.

She shook her head. "No. For the most part, I'm pleased

THE MISPLACED MISS ELOISE

with the changes I'm making. But it's all so much. It's all so new. I don't know who to trust."

"You don't know if you trust yourself," he said.

She gaped at him. "Yes. Yes, that's it exactly. How did you know?"

He smiled. "I know you and Charlotte better than you think. I've watched you grow up, haven't I?"

She nodded, leaning into his warmth. He wrapped an arm around her, glancing toward the salon where Alex waited. "You know he won't wait forever, don't you? I had to physically stop him from chasing after you. I told him to give me a moment, but..."

She laughed softly, her heart clenching at the thought of Alex rushing after her.

Of Alex turning back from his planned trip just to find her.

She bit her lip. Oh dear, she was definitely crying more than she liked.

Rodrick shook his head. "I never thought I'd see the day that Alex lost his head over a woman." He grinned down at her. "And I never would have guessed it would be you."

Lost his head.

She swallowed hard, still trying to digest his sudden reappearance. Still trying to understand what this meant.

No, that wasn't it. Truthfully, it was fear at work inside her. Fear that she'd be hurt again. Fear that she was being swept up in something too powerful to control. Fear that at the end of it all she'd be back to being the old Eloise. Not belonging to herself but to someone else.

Because whenever she was near Alex, she was in danger of losing herself.

She bit her lip as her chest tightened.

She was in danger of losing her heart.

"El, when you ran off the night before your wedding,"

Rodrick started slowly. "I was worried about you, obviously, but also...a little proud, if I'm being honest."

She sniffed, looking up at her brother.

"I was even prouder when you chose to come back here and face our parents and your troubles. That's not easy. It took courage." He reached up to touch her cheek. "Don't stop now."

She pressed her lips together to hold back a sob. The emotions that had sprung up at seeing Alex were so overwhelming it was terrifying.

"He clearly loves you," Rodrick continued gently. "And that is rare in our world. Tell him how you feel."

She stared at her brother for a long moment, turning over his words...and then a short laugh escaped.

"What's so funny?" he asked.

"It's just..." She threw her hands out. "You lecturing me on being open and honest with my feelings."

His brow furrowed in confusion.

She tilted her head to the side, her voice tentative. "Don't you think that perhaps you ought to follow your own advice?"

He sighed. "El..."

"I know you love Franny, but does she know?"

"That's different," he said, his voice clipped.

"Is it? Because I don't see how—"

"Franny and I are friends. If I were to tell her..." He looked away. "It would change things. It could ruin everything."

She wanted to argue but his expression grew shuttered. "Besides, we're not talking about me. The person I love isn't mere feet away waiting for a response." He arched his brows. "The person I love didn't just declare their love for me."

The person I love...

Did she love him? Was that what this was?

Her head spun with questions.

But the answers wouldn't be found out here with Rodrick. She took a deep breath and nodded, but before she could speak, Alex's voice came from the doorway behind them.

"All right, look, I waited as long as I could." Irritation and impatience had his voice short and curt.

Eloise had the most ridiculous urge to laugh as she turned to face him. She had an even more overpowering urge to go to him. To throw her arms around him and hold him tight.

Rodrick looked between them, but his words were for Eloise. "I'll be just inside the door if you need me."

She nodded, but her gaze never left Alex's as Rodrick moved past him to give them some privacy.

His eyes were filled with so many emotions, it made her heart shout and cheer and weep in turn. "You hurt me," she finally said.

His expression was pained as he moved closer. "I know. And I'm sorry. When I sent that message, I told myself it was for your own good. I should have told you, I know that. I handled it all wrong."

"I handled everything all wrong too," she admitted.

He was so close now she could feel his warmth. "The more time we spent together, the more frightened I became."

Her brows arched. "You? Frightened?"

He nodded. "You were right when you called me out for running away as well. My parents might be gone, but I was running from the past. Trying to avoid repeating their mistakes by avoiding my responsibilities and..." He shrugged. "And my life."

Her heart ached at the openness in his eyes. That sardonic humor and the gruff manners were gone, leaving Alex. Flawed and imperfect, but...perfect all the same. Perfectly human, and just as confused as Eloise.

"I thought that if I could avoid feeling deeply for someone, then I wouldn't have to worry about being the cruel, possessive man my father had become. I suppose I thought that if I didn't marry, I could never hurt a woman like my mother was hurt." He shook his head. "It makes no sense—"

"No," she interrupted. "It does. I...I understand. It's difficult to know the way forward when you don't have an example to follow."

Her mind strayed to her own parents. They might have had the best of intentions, but it was as though they'd both lost sight of what was important. And they seemed to encourage the worst in each other in that sense.

"I'd spent so long trying to make everyone else happy, trying to please people as if that might make them love me..." She swallowed, her gaze locked on his. "But honestly, loving someone and being loved, it's...it's frightening. It's...it's unknown."

He nodded, more serious than she'd ever seen him. "It's terrifying."

Her shoulders slumped with a relief that she could hardly explain. But the fact that he admitted it, and that he was just as confused and overwhelmed...

"How do you understand me so well?" she asked.

He shook his head. "I wondered the same about you. I've never met someone who made me feel like..." He put a hand to his chest, his jaw working like he was struggling to find the words. "Who made me feel like I fit. Like I belong. I don't want to lose that."

She shook her head. "Me neither. But...but I'm scared. I don't want to lose myself again. I'm just starting to figure out who I am and what I want and..."

He nodded when she didn't finish. "And you don't want some highhanded earl coming along and swallowing you whole."

Tears slid down her cheeks because, "Honestly, how do

you do that? How do you know me so well when we've only just met?"

"I think perhaps we're more alike than we'd thought," he said slowly. "I know now, finally, what it is that I want. What I need."

Her breath hitched. "What's that?"

His lips twitched and she felt an echoing thump in her chest. "I need a knight in shining armor."

Her eyes widened and then her head fell back with a laugh as she remembered her story, about how she'd wanted to be a knight. "You don't need a knight."

"I do," he insisted. He was smiling now, but it wasn't teasing, just filled with affection as he reached out and drew her into his arms. "You alone helped me to realize my fears and face them. If that's not a knight, I don't know what is."

A smile tugged at her lips as well. "Then I suppose I could say the same about you. Being with you helped me to realize that running away isn't the answer. That I need to stay and fight for the life that I want."

He nodded slowly and the depth of emotions in his eyes made her knees go weak. "El, what you want..." He cleared his throat, his arms tightening around her waist. "The life you talked about when we were together... The family and the love and the laughter...I want that. I want that with you."

Tears spilled over as her lips quivered. She could see it. She could see it so clearly it was as if it had always been Alex in her dreams. As if she'd known it was him even before they'd met.

Silly and fantastical...but that was how it felt.

"I want that too," she whispered.

She'd no sooner said the words then his lips were crushing hers in a bruising kiss. Heat seared through her as he groaned with relief. His warm, firm lips guided hers in a kiss that made her belly tighten and her limbs grow heavy.

She forgot entirely that she was outside in the night air as his heat wrapped around her just as surely as his arms.

"I love you, El," he whispered.

"I love you too." His face was wet from her tears and he grinned when she reached up to swipe them away. "What now?" she asked.

"Now we...we take it one step at a time," he said.

At her arched brows, his smile broadened, his eyes glinting with joy. "We have time, El, and the last thing I want is for you to feel pressured or uncertain."

"I don't," she started. "Feel pressured, that is. Or uncertain."

He kissed her. "I want to get to know you. The real you. The you you're becoming."

She nodded, happiness making it impossible not to beam from ear to ear. "And I want to get to know you too. All of you, the good and the bad."

He leaned down until his lips grazed hers. "So, we are courting then."

"We are," she agreed on a sigh.

"You know, if this were a traditional courtship, I should really be keeping my distance right now," he murmured.

"Mmm." A mischievous grin tugged at her lips. "We agreed we're courting. No one said it would be traditional."

He laughed. "I think perhaps we forsook tradition when you snuck into my luggage."

She was still giggling when he claimed her lips for another kiss.

"I do love you, Alex," she said when he lifted his head.

His eyes danced with laughter and his lips twitched with amusement. "And I love you, my darling."

EPILOGUE

Two months later...

THE CARRIAGE WAITED in front of the new Lord Pickington's estate, along with the newly married couple's closest family and friends.

"Oh, I do so hate goodbyes," her mother said before kissing her cheek and departing with her father.

For the best, as the rest of her friends were not nearly as decorous with their tearful farewells.

"Give Charlotte my love," Mary said through her tears as she gave Eloise a crushing hug.

"I will," Eloise promised. "We will be meeting up with her in Paris. I can only imagine how much our dear Charlotte is enjoying the French culture."

Mary laughed as she swiped at her eyes. "She will be ecstatic to see you..." She arched her brows meaningfully. "And to see you so happy."

Mary's new husband, Lord Paul, wrapped an arm around his wife's shoulders. "There, there, love. You still have me."

She swatted his chest playfully and soon they were lost in their own world of whispered jests and laughter.

"You know the first thing Charlotte will do is tease you," Rodrick said. He was standing with Alex, Franny on his other side.

Eloise grinned. "Oh, I know it. She will never let me forget that I somehow managed to avoid marrying Pickington...but still somehow ended up as Lady Pickington."

Alex shrugged good-naturedly. "I did not choose the title. The title chose me."

Eloise found it hard to tear her gaze away from her handsome husband. When his eyes were on her like this, so filled with tenderness, laughter, and affection...it was hard to do anything but swoon.

Not that she ever swooned. Of course she didn't.

But she'd never deny that she'd gone and fallen head over heels for her husband. The only man who made her feel like she was home whenever she was with him. He encouraged her, and supported her, and respected her wishes.

But most of all...he loved her. He made her feel more cherished and wanted and seen than she'd ever imagined possible.

After a long, lingering, love-filled look, she finally tore her gaze away. They had an entire trip to the continent during which she could gaze upon him to her heart's content. But for now, there were goodbyes to be said.

The hardest farewell was with Lydia.

The sweet redhead was ensconced by Mary and Paul on one side and Miss Farthington on the other. She was in good hands, Eloise knew, but she still felt a surge of protectiveness.

Lydia seemed to sense it because when Eloise leaned in to

embrace her, Lydia whispered. "Do not concern yourself with me. Enjoy yourself. You deserve it."

Eloise leaned back to smile at her friend, but she reached for her hands and gripped them. "You will be all right on your own?"

"She's hardly on her own," Miss Farthington said with a laugh as she wrapped an arm around Lydia's waist.

Mary grinned. "Indeed not. Lydia will be tired of our company by the time you return."

Lydia laughed, but her gaze was understanding. "I will be fine, Eloise. Please, don't worry. In fact, I've decided that you are my new role model."

Eloise's eyes widened. "Me?"

"Yes. You've been so brave and have grown so much over the months I've known you," Lydia said. "I should like to do the same. So go, enjoy your journey, and know that you have been a good influence."

"Just so long as you don't run away," Miss Farthington teased. "My heart could not take it if one of my charges went missing."

"Oh no," Lydia said, more earnest than necessary considering Miss Farthington's joking tone. "I would never dare to run off on my own. But..." She tilted her chin up. "I should like to overcome my shyness. Somehow."

"And you will, dear," Mary said.

"Eloise," Rodrick interrupted, coming to her side to draw her into an embrace. "Franny and I will miss you terribly."

Alex clapped Rodrick on the shoulder. "We will be back before you know it. And we'll look forward to hearing all about your wedding."

Franny brightened at the mention of their wedding as she kissed Eloise's cheek. "Rodrick is right, you know. You will be missed."

Eloise squeezed her soon-to-be sister-in-law's hand with

a smile. Franny was standing close to Rodrick's side but something about their stiff postures made Eloise think that Rodrick hadn't yet confessed.

She had half a mind to nag him about it—she wanted nothing more than to see Rodrick as happy as she and Charlotte were. But before she could, Alex was wrapping an arm about her waist and steering her toward the carriage.

They were waving and shouting their farewells as Alex helped her in.

Once inside and blissfully alone, Alex wasted no time pulling her into his lap where she snuggled into his chest.

"There now," he said with a contented growl. "If we'd traveled like this the first time, we'd have been far more comfortable on the journey."

Eloise laughed. "If we'd traveled like this the first time, you would have had to marry me right then and there."

He pulled back his head to grin down at her. "Would that have been so terrible?"

She pursed her lips to mull it over. "No, not terrible," she said slowly. "But I'm glad we waited. It was horrible being apart from you, but I'm glad we entered into this marriage on our terms."

"Mmm," he murmured, leaning down to kiss the tip of her nose. "Agreed. It may have taken longer, but I'm glad there were no misunderstandings or confusion between us."

She sighed contentedly as she wrapped her arms around his neck. Their courtship hadn't been long, by anyone's standards, but it had been long enough for them to get to know one another the way they ought.

They talked about everything and anything over the weeks they were courting. By the time the betrothal was official, she knew the lengths he'd taken to rid himself of the wounds his parents had left behind. And with his help, she sorted through her own remaining qualms with her parents and had decided to forgive them their heavy-handed ways, so they might all move on with a new relationship founded on more equal footing.

In the days leading up to the wedding, they'd left the past behind and had focused on the future instead.

"I feel like I've been waiting forever for this journey," Eloise said.

"Are you certain you wish to stay at the same inn?" he asked, amusement twinkling in his eyes the way she so adored. "I'm afraid the innkeeper's wife will have much to say about us returning and sharing a room."

Eloise laughed. "Let her say what she will." She arched her brows. "I think it's romantic to retrace our steps."

He leaned in until his nose grazed hers and his smiling lips were a breath away from hers. "Whatever you say, wife. I am happy to follow you wherever you wish to go. Just so long as by the end of it, you are at my side."

"Always," she whispered.

His kiss was sweet and gentle. The mark of a new beginning. And as their carriage moved into motion, and his arms wrapped around her tighter still, she knew that a beginning was exactly what this was.

For they had a long future ahead of them. A new path that they'd forge together. A new family that they couldn't wait to create. And a love that would sustain them all for a lifetime.

* * *

THANKS FOR READING! Be sure to check out Miss Lydia's story next in *The Mysterious Miss Lydia*, available at https://maggiedallenbooks.com

. . .

Curious about what happens to Rodrick and Franny? Read their short romance in the prequel for the upcoming School of Charm series spinoff, Charmed by Chance.

ABOUT THE AUTHOR

MAGGIE DALLEN IS a big city girl living in Montana. She writes romantic comedies in a range of genres including young adult, historical, and contemporary. An unapologetic addict of all things romance, she loves to connect with fellow avid readers. Subscribe to her historical newsletter at http://eepurl.com/dgUNif

Printed in Great Britain
by Amazon